THE CHILDREN'S ILLUSTRATED TREASURY OF CHRISTMAS CAROLS & STORIES

hinkler

THIS BOOK BELONGS TO

....

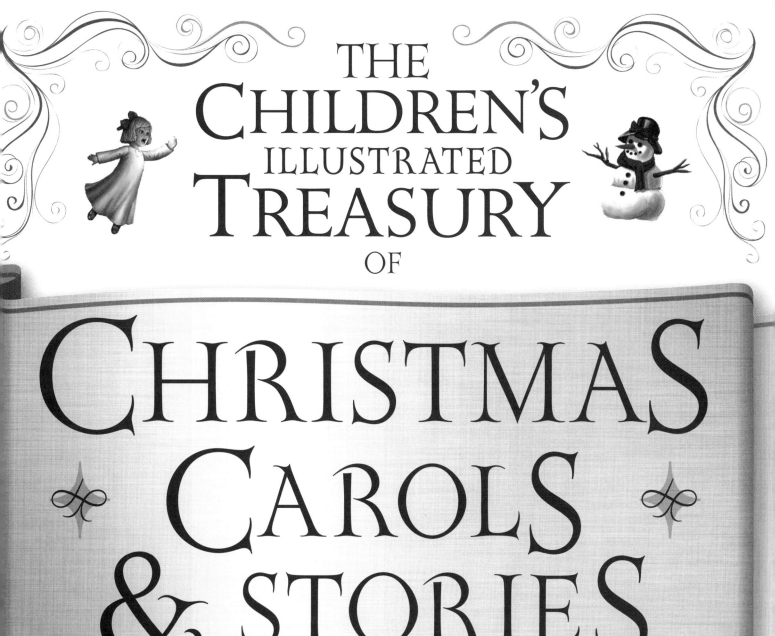

THE CHILDREN'S ILLUSTRATED TREASURY OF

CHRISTMAS CAROLS & STORIES

Published by Hinkler Books Pty Ltd
45–55 Fairchild Street
Heatherton Victoria 3202 Australia
www.hinkler.com.au

hinkler

© Hinkler Books Pty Ltd 2010, 2015

Editor: Suzannah Pearce
Cover design: Sam Grimmer
Internal design: Trudi Webb
Illlustrators: Brijbasi Art Press Ltd, Suzie Byrne, Graphics Manufacture, Melissa Webb
Prepress: Graphic Print Group

ISBN 978 1 7428 1969 3

Printed and bound in China

CONTENTS

THE MAGIC OF CHRISTMAS

JINGLE BELLS

Words by James Lord Pierpont

Dashing through the snow
In a one-horse open sleigh,
O'er the fields we go,
Laughing all the way.
Bells on bobtail ring,
Making spirits bright,
What fun it is to laugh and sing
A sleighing song tonight.

Chorus

Jingle bells, jingle bells,
Jingle all the way;
Oh what fun it is to ride
In a one-horse open sleigh.
Jingle bells, jingle bells,
Jingle all the way;
Oh what fun it is to ride
In a one-horse open sleigh.

A day or two ago,
I thought I'd take a ride
And soon, Miss Fanny Bright
Was seated by my side,
The horse was lean and lank,
Misfortune seemed his lot,
He got into a drifted bank,
And then we got upsot.

Chorus

8

A day or two ago,
The story I must tell,
I went out on the snow,
And on my back I fell;
A gent was riding by
In a one-horse open sleigh,
He laughed as there I sprawling lie,
But quickly drove away.

Chorus

Now the ground is white,
Go it while you're young,
Take the girls tonight,
And sing this sleighing song;
Just get a bobtailed bay,
Two forty as his speed,
Hitch him to an open sleigh
And crack! You'll take the lead.

Chorus

UP ON THE HOUSETOP

Words by Benjamin Hanby

Up on the housetop reindeer pause,
Out jumps good old Santa Claus.
Down through the chimney with lots of toys,
All for the little ones, Christmas joys.

Chorus

Ho, ho, ho! Who wouldn't go!
Ho, ho, ho! Who wouldn't go!
Up on the housetop, click, click, click,
Down through the chimney with good Saint Nick.

First comes the stocking of little Nell;
Oh, dear Santa, fill it well;
Give her a dolly that laughs and cries,
One that will open and shut her eyes.

Chorus

Next comes the stocking of little Will;
Oh, just see what a glorious fill!
Here is a hammer and lots of tacks,
Whistle and ball and a set of jacks.

Chorus

SAINT NICK

Written by M. Nora Boylan

When cold the winds blow,
And comes the white snow,
Then look out for good Saint Nick.
He comes in a sleigh
From miles, miles away,
And vanishes very quick.

S is for Santa

Written by W. S. C.

S stands for stockings we hang up so high.
A is for all we get if we don't cry.
N is for nobody he will pass by.
T is for tomorrow – the day we eat pie.
A stands for at last old Santa is nigh.

C for the children who love him so well.
L for the little girl, his name she can spell.
A stands for apples so rosy and red.
U is for us as we wait for his sled.
S stands for Santa Claus, who
comes in the night, when we
are tucked up in bed with our
eyes closed so tight.

ONCE A YEAR

Written by Thomas Tusser

At Christmas play and make good cheer,
For Christmas comes but once a year.

SANTA'S HELPERS

Written by M. Nora Boylan

The fairies and brownies on last Christmastide
  Decided to open their hearts very wide,
And spend extra time, throughout the whole year,
In helping their grandfather – Santa Claus dear.

'Our fingers are nimble. We'll quickly make toys
Enough to supply all the girls and the boys,
And Santa may watch us to see if it's right,
So all will be ready before Christmas night.'

Then bravely they all went to work with a will,
And soon all was quiet in workshop and mill;
For old Santa said, 'Enough, and well done,
We've toys enough now to make all kinds of fun.'

We thank you, old Santa, and your helpers, too,
For all of the many kind things that you do;
And should you need more help in making your toys,
Just call on your small friends, the girls and the boys.

THE GIFT OF THE MAGI

Adapted from the story written by O. Henry

One dollar and eighty-seven cents. That was all. Three times Della counted it. One dollar and eighty-seven cents. And the next day would be Christmas. There was clearly nothing to do but flop down on the shabby little couch and howl. So Della did it.

When Della finished her cry she powdered her cheeks. She stood by the window and looked out at a grey cat walking along a grey fence in a grey backyard. Tomorrow would be Christmas Day, and she had only $1.87 with which to buy her husband Jim a present. She had been saving every penny she could for months, with this result. Only $1.87 to buy a present for Jim. Her Jim. Many a happy hour she had spent planning for something nice for him. Something fine and rare.

There was a large, high mirror between the windows of the room. Suddenly Della whirled from the window and stood before the mirror. Her eyes were shining brilliantly, but her face had lost its colour. Rapidly she pulled down her hair and let it fall to its full length.

Now, there were two possessions in which Della and Jim both took a mighty pride. One was Jim's gold watch that had been his father's and his grandfather's. The other was Della's hair. Della's beautiful hair fell about her, rippling and shining like a cascade of brown waters. It reached below her knees and made itself almost a garment for her. And then she did it up again, nervously and quickly.

On went her old brown jacket; on went her old brown hat. With a whirl of her skirts and with the brilliant sparkle still in her eyes, she fluttered out the door and down the stairs to the street.

She stopped at a shop with a sign that read: 'Madame Sofronie, Hair Goods of All Kinds.' One flight up Della ran, then collected herself, panting.

'Will you buy my hair?' asked Della.

'I buy hair,' said Madame. 'Take yer hat off and let's have a look at it.'

Della let down her hair.

'Twenty dollars,' said Madame, lifting Della's hair and examining it closely.

'Give it to me quick,' said Della.

The next two hours tripped by on rosy wings. Della searched the stores for Jim's present.

She found it at last. It surely had been made for Jim and no one else. There was no other like it in any of the stores, and she had turned all of them inside out. It was a platinum fob chain, simple in design, declaring its value by substance alone and not by being showy. It was even worthy of The Watch. As soon as she saw it she knew that it must be Jim's. It was like him. Quiet and valuable — the description applied to both. Twenty-one dollars they took from her for it, and she hurried home with the eighty-seven cents. With that chain on his watch Jim might be properly anxious about the time in any company. Grand as the watch was, he sometimes looked at it on the sly on account of the old leather strap he used in place of a chain.

When Della reached home, she got out her curling irons and lighted the gas and went to work repairing her hair. Within forty minutes her head was covered with tiny close-lying curls that made her look wonderfully like a truant schoolboy. She looked at her reflection in the mirror long, carefully and critically.

'If Jim doesn't kill me,' she said to herself, 'before he takes a second look at me, he'll say I look like a Coney Island chorus girl. But what could I do? Oh, what could I do with a dollar and eighty-seven cents?'

At seven o'clock the coffee was made and the frying pan was hot on the back of the stove.

Jim was never late. Della doubled the fob chain in her hand and sat on the corner of the table near the door that he always entered. Then she heard his step on the stair down on the first flight, and she turned white for just a moment. She had a habit of saying little silent prayers about the simplest everyday things, and now she whispered, 'Please, God, make him think I am still pretty.'

The door opened and Jim stepped in and closed it. He looked thin and very serious. He needed a new overcoat and he was without gloves.

Jim stopped inside the door. His eyes were fixed upon Della. There was an expression in them that she could not read, and it terrified her. It was not anger, nor surprise, nor disapproval, nor horror, nor any of the sentiments that she had been prepared for. He simply stared at her fixedly with that peculiar expression on his face.

'Jim, darling,' Della cried, 'don't look at me that way. I had my hair cut off and sold it because I couldn't live through Christmas without giving you a present. It'll grow out again. My hair grows awfully fast. Say "Merry Christmas" Jim, and let's be happy. You don't know what a beautiful gift I've got for you.'

'You've cut off your hair?' asked Jim in confusion.

'Cut it off and sold it,' said Della. 'Don't you like me just as well, anyhow? I'm me without my hair, ain't I?'

Jim looked about the room curiously.

'You say your hair is gone?' he asked again.

'You needn't look for it,' said Della. 'It's sold, I tell you. It's Christmas Eve. Maybe the hairs of my head were numbered,' she went on with a sudden serious sweetness, 'but nobody could ever count my love for you.'

Out of his trance Jim seemed quickly to wake. He embraced his Della.

Then Jim drew a package from his overcoat pocket.

'Don't make any mistake, Dell,' he said. 'A haircut couldn't make me like my girl any less. But if you'll unwrap that package, you may see why you had me going a while at first.'

Her fingers nimbly tore at the string and paper. There was an ecstatic scream of joy, which quickly changed to hysterical tears and wails.

For there lay The Combs — the set of combs that Della had worshipped for so long in a Broadway window. Beautiful combs — pure tortoiseshell with jewelled rims. They were expensive combs, and her heart had simply yearned for them without the least hope of owning them. And now they were hers, but the tresses they should have adorned were gone.

But she hugged them, and at length she was able to look up with a smile and say, 'My hair grows so fast, Jim!'

And then Della leaped up and cried, 'Oh, Oh!'

Jim had not yet seen his beautiful present.

Della held out the chain to him eagerly upon her open palm. The precious metal seemed to flash with a reflection of her bright spirit.

'Isn't it a dandy, Jim? I hunted all over town to find it. You'll have to look at the time a hundred times a day now. Give me your watch. I want to see how it looks on it.'

Instead of obeying, Jim tumbled down on the couch and put his hand under the back of his head and smiled.

'Dell,' said he, 'let's put our Christmas presents away and keep 'em a while. They're too nice to use just now. I sold the watch to get the money to buy your combs!'

The magi were wise men – wonderfully wise men – who brought gifts to the Babe in the manger. They invented the art of giving Christmas presents. Being wise, their gifts were no doubt wise ones. And here I have related to you the uneventful tale of two foolish people who most unwisely sacrificed for each other the greatest treasures of their home. But in a last word, let it be said that of all who give gifts these two were the wisest. And all who give and receive gifts are the wisest. They are the magi.

A Christmas Lullaby

From Christmas Entertainments *by Alice M. Kellogg, author unknown*
Sing to the tune of the carol Silent Night

Hushaby, hushaby,
Christmas stars are in the sky;
Sweet the bells of Christmas Eve –
Babies, each a kiss receive –
Hushaby, goodnight,
Hushaby, goodnight!

Lullaby, lullaby,
Babies in their cradles lie;
Every one in white is gowned,
Hush, make not a single sound!
Lullaby, goodnight,
Lullaby, goodnight!

Rockaby, rockaby,
Christmastide draweth nigh;
Quiet now the tiny feet,
Babies sleep so still and sweet –
Sweetest dreams, goodnight,
Sweetest dreams, goodnight!

SANTA CLAUS

From The Treasure Book of Children's Verse, author unknown

He comes in the night! He comes in the night!
He softly, silently comes;
While the little brown heads on the pillows so white
Are dreaming of bugles and drums.
He cuts through the snow like a ship through the foam,
While the white flakes around him whirl;
Who tells him I know not, but he finds the home
Of each good little boy and girl.

His sleigh it is long, and deep, and wide;
It will carry a host of things,
While dozens of drums hang over the side,
With the sticks sticking under the strings.
And yet not the sound of a drum is heard,
Not a bugle blast is blown,
As he mounts to the chimney-top like a bird,
And drops to the hearth like a stone.

The little red stockings he silently fills,
Till the stockings will hold no more;
The bright little sleds for the great snow hills
Are quickly set down on the floor.
Then Santa Claus mounts to the roof like a bird,
And glides to his seat in the sleigh;
Not a sound of a bugle or drum is heard,
As he noiselessly gallops away.

He rides to the east, and he rides to the west,
Of his goodies he touches not one;
He eats the crumbs of the Christmas feast
When the dear little folks are done.
Old Santa Claus does all that he can;
This beautiful mission is his;
Then, children be good to the little old man,
When you find who the little man is.

YES, VIRGINIA, THERE IS A SANTA CLAUS

In 1897, a girl called Virginia wrote a letter to the Editor of The Sun newspaper in New York. On 21 September, her letter was printed in the newspaper, with a reply from the Editor, Francis Pharcellus Church.

Dear Editor,

I am 8 years old. Some of my little friends say there is no Santa Claus. Papa says, 'If you see it in The Sun it's so.' Please tell me the truth; is there a Santa Claus?

Virginia O'Hanlon
115 West Ninety-fifth Street

Is There a Santa Claus?

DEAR EDITOR, I am 8 years old.

Some of my little friends say there is no Santa Claus. Papa says, If you see it in THE SUN it's so. Please tell me the truth; is there a Santa Claus?

VIRGINIA O'HANLON
115 WEST NINETY-FIFTH STREET

VIRGINIA, your little friends are wrong. They have been affected by the skepticism of a skeptical age. They do not believe except they see. They think that nothing can be which is not comprehensible by their little minds. All minds, VIRGINIA, whether they be men's or children's, are little. In this great universe of ours man is a mere insect, an ant, in his intellect, as compared with the boundless world about him, as measured by the intelligence capable of grasping the whole of truth and knowledge.

Yes, VIRGINIA, there is a Santa Claus. He exists as certainly as love and generosity and devotion exist, and you know that they abound and give to your life its highest beauty and joy. Alas! How dreary would be the world if there were no Santa Claus. It would be as dreary as if there were no VIRGINIAS. There would be no childlike faith then, no poetry, no romance to make tolerable this existence. We should have no enjoyment, except in sense and sight. The eternal light with which childhood fills the world would be extinguished.

Not believe in Santa Claus! You might as well not believe in fairies! You might get your papa to hire men to watch in all the chimneys on Christmas Eve to catch Santa Claus, but even if they did not see Santa Claus coming down, what would that prove? Nobody sees Santa Claus, but that is no sign that there is no Santa Claus. The most real things in the world are those that neither children nor men can see. Did you ever see fairies dancing on the lawn? Of course not, but that's no proof that they are not there. Nobody can conceive or imagine all the wonders there are unseen and unseeable in the world.

h leads people
 make a living,
ve in all cases.
s the driving
gth of time is
embers.

mes the wheel
 grist to grind.
 Colonisation
 Connecticut
s, and pay his
good hotel.

You may tear apart the baby's rattle and see what makes the noise inside, but there is a veil covering the unseen world which not the strongest man, nor even the united strength of all the strongest men that ever lived, could tear apart. Only faith, fancy, poetry, love, romance, can push aside that curtain and view and picture the supernal beauty and glory beyond. Is it all real? Ah, VIRGINIA, in all this world there is nothing else real and abiding.

No Santa Claus! Thank God! He lives, and he lives forever. A thousand years from now, VIRGINIA, nay, ten times ten thousand years from now, he will continue to make glad the heart of childhood.

DING DONG MERRILY ON HIGH

Words by George Woodward

Ding dong! Merrily on high
In heav'n the bells are ringing,
Ding dong! Verily the sky
Is riv'n with angel singing.

Chorus

Gloria,
Hosanna in excelsis!

E'en so here below, below,
Let steeple bells be swungen,
And 'Io, io, io!'
By priest and people sungen.

Chorus

Pray you, dutifully prime
Your matin chime, ye ringers;
May you beautifully rime
Your evetime song, ye singers.

Chorus

CHRISTMAS GREETINGS
(FROM A FAIRY TO A CHILD)

Written by Lewis Carroll

Lady dear, if Fairies may
    For a moment lay aside
Cunning tricks and elfish play,
    'Tis at happy Christmastide.

We have heard the children say —
    Gentle children, whom we love —
Long ago, on Christmas Day,
    Came a message from above.

Still, as Christmastide comes round,
    They remember it again —
Echo still the joyful sound
    'Peace on earth, goodwill to men!'

Yet the hearts must childlike be
    Where such heavenly guests abide:
Unto children, in their glee,
    All the year is Christmastide!

Thus, forgetting tricks and play
    For a moment, Lady dear,
We would wish you, if we may,
    Merry Christmas, glad New Year!

DECK
THE
HALLS

O CHRISTMAS TREE

Traditional German carol

O Christmas tree! O Christmas tree!
Thy leaves are so unchanging;
O Christmas tree! O Christmas tree!
Thy leaves are so unchanging;
Not only green when summer's here,
But also when 'tis cold and drear.
O Christmas tree! O Christmas tree!
Thy leaves are so unchanging!

O Christmas tree! O Christmas tree!
Much pleasure thou can'st give me;
O Christmas tree! O Christmas tree!
Much pleasure thou can'st give me;
How often has the Christmas tree
Afforded me the greatest glee!
O Christmas tree! O Christmas tree!
Much pleasure thou can'st give me.

O Christmas tree! O Christmas tree!
Thy candles shine so brightly!
O Christmas tree! O Christmas tree!
Thy candles shine so brightly!
From base to summit, gay and bright,
There's only splendour for the sight.
O Christmas tree! O Christmas tree!
Thy candles shine so brightly!

O Christmas tree! O Christmas tree!
How richly God has decked thee!
O Christmas tree! O Christmas tree!
How richly God has decked thee!
Thou bidst us true and faithful be,
And trust in God unchangingly.
O Christmas tree! O Christmas tree!
How richly God has decked thee!

THE FOOLISH FIR TREE

Written by Henry van Dyke

A tale that the poet Rückert told
To German children, in days of old;
Disguised in a random, rollicking rhyme
Like a merry actor of ancient time,
And sent, in its English dress, to please
The little folk of the Christmas trees.

A little fir grew in the midst of the wood
Contented and happy, as young trees should.
His body was straight and his boughs were clean;
And summer and winter the bountiful sheen
Of his needles bedecked him, from top to root,
In a beautiful, all-the-year, evergreen suit.

But a trouble came into his heart one day,
When he saw that the other trees were gay
In the wonderful garment that summer weaves
Of numerous shapes and kinds of leaves:
He looked at his needles so stiff and small,
And thought that his dress was the poorest of all.
Then jealousy clouded the little tree's mind,
And he said to himself, 'It was not very kind
To give such an ugly old dress to a tree!
If the forest fairies would only ask me,
I'd tell them how I should like to be dressed,
In a garment of gold, to bedazzle the rest!'
So he fell asleep, but his dreams were bad.
When he woke in the morning, his heart was glad;
For every leaf that his boughs could hold
Was made of the brightest beaten gold.
I tell you, children, the tree was proud;
He was something above the common crowd;
And he tinkled his leaves, as if he would say
To a peddler who happened to pass that way,
'Just look at me! Don't you think I am fine?
And wouldn't you like such a dress as mine?'
'Oh, yes!' said the man, 'and I really guess
I must fill my pack with your beautiful dress.'
So he picked the golden leaves with care,
And left the little tree shivering there.

'Oh, why did I wish for golden leaves?'
The fir tree said, 'I forgot that thieves
Would be sure to rob me in passing by.
If the fairies would give me another try,
I'd wish for something that cost much less,
And be satisfied with glass for my dress!'
Then he fell asleep; and, just as before,
The fairies granted his wish once more.
When the night was gone, and the sun rose clear,
The tree was a crystal chandelier;
And it seemed, as he stood in the morning light,
That his branches were covered with jewels bright.
'Aha!' said the tree. 'This is something great!'
And he held himself up, very proud and straight;
But a rude young wind through the forest dashed,
In a reckless temper, and quickly smashed
The delicate leaves. With a clashing sound
They broke into pieces and fell on the ground,
Like a silvery, shimmering shower of hail,
And the tree stood naked and bare to the gale.

Then his heart was sad, and he cried, 'Alas
For my beautiful leaves of shining glass!
Perhaps I have made another mistake
In choosing a dress so easy to break.
If the fairies only would hear me again
I'd ask them for something both pretty and plain:
It wouldn't cost much to grant my request,
In leaves of green lettuce I'd like to be dressed!'
By this time the fairies were laughing, I know;
But they gave him his wish in a second; and so
With leaves of green lettuce, all tender and sweet,
The tree was arrayed, from his head to his feet.
'I knew it!' he cried, 'I was sure I could find
The sort of a suit that would be to my mind.
There's none of the trees has a prettier dress,
And none as attractive as I am, I guess.'
But a goat, who was taking an afternoon walk,
By chance overheard the fir tree's talk.
So he came up close for a nearer view;
'My salad!' he bleated, 'I think so too!
You're the most attractive kind of a tree,
And I want your leaves for my five-o'clock tea.'
So he ate them all without saying grace,
And walked away with a grin on his face;
While the little tree stood in the twilight dim,
With never a leaf on a single limb.

Then he sighed and groaned; but his voice was weak—
He was so ashamed that he could not speak.
He knew at last he had been a fool,
To think of breaking the forest rule,
And choosing a dress himself to please,
Because he envied the other trees.
But it couldn't be helped, it was now too late,
He must make up his mind to a leafless fate!
So he let himself sink in a slumber deep,
But he moaned and he tossed in his troubled sleep,
Till the morning touched him with joyful beam,
And he woke to find it was all a dream.
For there in his evergreen dress he stood,
A pointed fir in the midst of the wood!
His branches were sweet with the fragrant smell,
His needles were green when the white snow fell.
And always contented and happy was he,
The very best kind of a Christmas tree.

DECK THE HALLS

Traditional Welsh carol

Deck the halls with boughs
of holly,
Fa la la la la, la la la la.
'Tis the season to be jolly,
Fa la la la la, la la la la.
Don we now our gay apparel,
Fa la la, la la la, la la la.
Troll the ancient yuletide carol,
Fa la la la la, la la la la.

See the blazing yule before us,
Fa la la la la, la la la la.
Strike the harp and join the chorus,
Fa la la la la, la la la la.
Follow me in merry measure,
Fa la la, la la la, la la la.
While I tell of yuletide treasure,
Fa la la la la, la la la la.

Fast away the old year passes,
Fa la la la la, la la la la.
Hail the new year, lads and lasses,
Fa la la la la, la la la la.
Sing we joyous, all together,
Fa la la, la la la, la la la.
Heedless of the wind and weather,
Fa la la la la, la la la la.

HANG UP THE BABY'S STOCKING

Written by Emily Huntington Miller

Hang up the baby's stocking:
Be sure you don't forget;
The dear little dimpled darling!
She ne'er saw Christmas yet;
But I've told her all about it,
And she opened her big blue eyes,
And I'm sure she understood it –
She looked so funny and wise.

Dear, what a tiny stocking!
It doesn't take much to hold
Such little pink toes as baby's
Away from the frost and cold.
But then for the baby's Christmas
It will never do at all;
Why, Santa wouldn't be looking
For anything half so small.

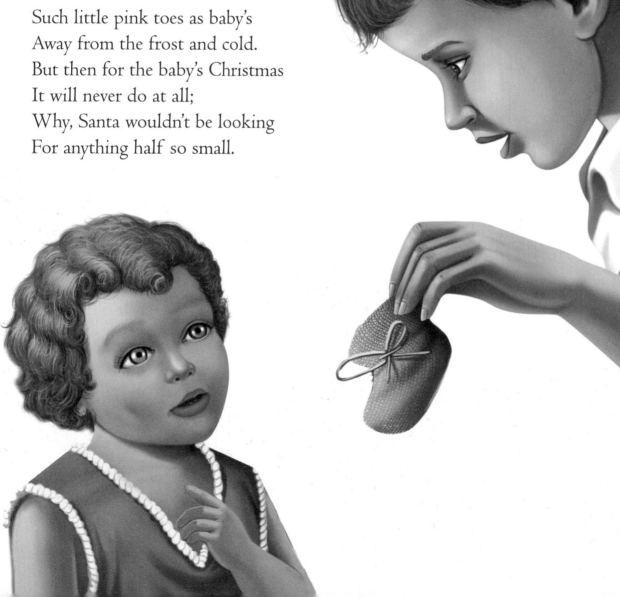

I know what will do for the baby.
I've thought of the very best plan:
I'll borrow a stocking from Grandma,
The longest that ever I can;
And you'll hang it by mine, dear Mother,
Right here in the corner, so!
And write a letter to Santa,
And fasten it on to the toe.

Write, 'This is the baby's stocking
That hangs in the corner here;
You never have seen her, Santa,
For she only came this year;
But she's just the blessedest baby!
And now, before you go,
Just cram her stocking with goodies,
From the top clean down to the toe.'

LITTLE GIRL'S CHRISTMAS

Adapted from the story written by Winnifred E. Lincoln

It was Christmas Eve, and Little Girl had just hung up her stocking by the fireplace – all ready for Santa when he slipped down the chimney. She knew he was coming, because – well, because it was Christmas Eve, and because he always had come to leave gifts for her on all the other Christmas Eves that she could remember.

Still, she wasn't satisfied. Way down in her heart she was a little uncertain. You see, when you have never really and truly seen a person with your very own eyes, it's hard to feel as if you exactly believe in him.

'Oh, he'll come,' said Little Girl. 'I just know he will be here before morning, but somehow I wish ... '

'Well, what do you wish?' said a tiny voice close by her – so close that Little Girl fairly jumped when she heard it.

'Why, I wish I could *see* Santa myself. I'd just like to go and see his house and his workshop, and ride in his sleigh, and meet Mrs Claus. It would be such fun, and then I'd *know* for sure.'

'Why don't you go, then?' said the tiny voice. 'It's easy enough. Just try on these shoes, and take this light in your hand, and you'll find your way all right.'

So Little Girl looked down on the hearth, and there were two little shoes side by side, and a little spark of a light close to them. Little Girl could hardly wait to pull off her slippers and try the shoes on. They looked as if they were too small, but they weren't – they fitted exactly right! Just as Little Girl had put them both on and had taken the light in her hand, along came a little breath of wind, and away she went up the chimney, along with ever so many other little sparks, past the soot fairies, and out into the open air, where Jack Frost and the star beams were busy making the world look pretty for Christmas.

Away went Little Girl – two shoes, bright light and all – higher and higher, until she looked like a star up in the sky. It was the funniest thing, but she seemed to know the way perfectly. You see, it was a straight road all the way, and when one doesn't have to think about turning to the right or the left, it makes things much easier. Pretty soon Little Girl noticed that there was a bright light all around her, and right away something down in her heart began to make her feel very happy indeed. She didn't know that the Christmas spirits and little Christmas fairies were all around her and even right inside her, because she couldn't see a single one of them.

Little Girl felt as if she wanted to laugh and sing and be glad. It made her remember the sick boy who lived next door, and she said to herself that she would take one of her prettiest picture books to him in the morning, so that he could have something to make him happy all day. By and by, when the bright light all around her had grown much brighter, Little Girl saw a path right in front of her, all straight and trim, leading up a hill to a big house with ever so many windows. When she had gone just a bit nearer, she saw candles in every window, red and green and yellow ones, and every one burning brightly, so Little Girl knew right away that these were Christmas candles to light her on her journey. Something told her that this was Santa's house, and that pretty soon she would perhaps see Santa himself.

Just as she neared the steps and before she could possibly have had time to ring the bell, the door opened itself as wide as could be. There stood – not Santa himself – but a funny little man with slender little legs and a roly-poly stomach, which shook every now and then when he laughed. You would have known right away, just as Little Girl knew, that he was a very happy little man, and you would have guessed right away, too, that the reason he was so roly-poly was because he laughed and chuckled and smiled all the time. Quick as a wink, he pulled off his little peaked red cap, smiled the broadest kind of a smile, and said, 'Merry Christmas! Merry Christmas! Come in! Come in!'

So in went Little Girl, holding fast to the little man's hand, and when she was really inside there was the jolliest, reddest fire all glowing and snapping, and there were the little man's brothers and sisters. They said their names were 'Merry Christmas', and 'Good Cheer', and ever so many other jolly-sounding things. There were so many of them that Little Girl just knew she never could count them, no matter how long she tried.

All around her were bundles and boxes and piles of toys and games, and Little Girl knew that these were all ready and waiting to be loaded into Santa's big sleigh. His reindeer would whirl them away over cloud-tops and snowdrifts to the little people down below who had left their stockings all ready for him. Pretty soon all the little Good Cheer brothers began to hurry and bustle and carry out the bundles as fast as they could to the steps where Little Girl could hear jingling bells and stamping hoofs. So Little Girl picked up some bundles and skipped along too, for she wanted to help a bit herself. There in the yard stood the *biggest* sleigh that Little Girl had ever seen. The reindeer were all stamping and prancing and jingling the bells on their harnesses, because they were so eager to be on their way around the earth once more.

She could hardly wait for Santa to come. Just as she had begun to wonder where he was, the door opened again and out came a whole forest of Christmas trees. At least, it looked just as if a whole forest had started out for a walk somewhere, but a second glance showed Little Girl that there were thousands of Christmas sprites, and that each one carried a tree or a big Christmas wreath on his back. Behind them all, she could hear someone laughing loudly, and talking in a big, jovial voice that sounded as if he were good friends with the whole world.

Straightaway she knew that Santa himself was coming. Little Girl's heart went pit-a-pat for a minute while she wondered if Santa would notice her. She didn't have to wonder long, for he spied her at once and said, 'Bless my soul! Who's this? And where did you come from?'

Little Girl thought perhaps she might be afraid to answer him, but she wasn't one bit afraid. You see he had such a kind little twinkle in his eyes that she felt happy right away as she replied, 'Oh, I'm Little Girl, and I wanted so much to see Santa that I just came, and here I am!'

'Ho, ho, ho, ho, ho!' laughed Santa, 'And here you are! Wanted to see Santa, did you, and so you came! Now that's very nice, and it's too bad I'm in such a hurry, for I should like nothing better than to show you about and give you a really good time. But you see it is quarter to twelve now, and I must be on my way at once, or else I'll never reach that first chimney-top by midnight. I'd call Mrs Claus and ask her to make you some supper, but she is busy finishing dolls' clothes, which must be done before morning. Is there anything that you would like, Little Girl?'

Santa put his big warm hand on Little Girl's head and she felt its warmth and kindness down to her very heart. You see, my dears, that even though Santa was in such a great hurry, he wasn't too busy to stop and make someone happy for a minute, even if it was someone no bigger than Little Girl.

So she smiled back into Santa's face and said, 'Oh, Santa, if I could only ride down with you behind those splendid reindeer! I'd love to go; won't you *please* take me? I'm so small that I won't take up much room on the seat, and I'll keep very still and not bother you one bit!'

Then Santa laughed *such* a laugh – big and loud and rollicking. He said, 'Wants a ride, does she? Well, well, shall we take her, little elves? Shall we take her, little fairies? Shall we take her, good reindeer?'

And all the little elves hopped and skipped and brought Little Girl a sprig of holly; and all the little fairies bowed and smiled and brought her a bit of mistletoe; and all the good reindeer jingled their bells loudly, which meant, 'Oh, yes! Let's take her!' And before Little Girl could even think, she found herself all tucked up in the big fur robes beside Santa. Away they went, right out into the air, over the clouds and on toward earth, whose lights Little Girl began to see twinkling away down below her. She knew that Santa would slip down a chimney in a minute. How she wanted to go, too!

So, just as Little Girl was wishing as hard as she could wish, she heard a tiny voice say, 'Hold tight to his arm! Hold tight to his arm!' So she held Santa's arm tight and close. Santa shouldered his pack and with a bound and a slide, they were right in the middle of a room where there was a fireplace and stockings.

Just then Santa noticed Little Girl. He had forgotten all about her for a minute, and he was very much surprised to find that she had come, too.

'Bless my soul!' Santa said. 'Where did you come from, Little Girl? And how in the world can we both get back up that chimney again? It's easy enough to slide down, but it's quite another matter to climb up again!' Santa looked worried.

But Little Girl was beginning to feel very tired by this time, for she had had a very exciting evening, so she said, 'Oh, never mind me, Santa. I've had such a good time, and I'd just as soon stay here a while as not. I believe I'll curl up on this hearth-rug a few minutes and have a little nap, for it looks as warm and cosy as our own hearth-rug at home, and — why, it is our own hearth and it's my own nursery, for there is Teddy Bear in his chair where I leave him every night.'

And Little Girl turned to thank Santa and say goodbye to him, but either he had gone very quickly, or else she had fallen asleep very quickly — she never could tell which — for the next thing she knew, Daddy was holding her in his arms and was saying, 'What is my Little Girl doing here? She must go to bed, for it's Christmas Eve, and old Santa won't come if he thinks there are any little folks about.'

But Little Girl knew better than that, and when she began to tell him all about it, and how the Christmas fairies had welcomed her, and how Santa had given her such a fine ride, Daddy laughed and said, 'You've been dreaming, my dear.'

But Little Girl knew better than that, too, for tight in her hand she held some holly berries which one of the Christmas elves had placed there. More than that, she had fallen asleep on the hearth-rug, just where Santa had left her, and that was the best proof of all.

HOLLY AND THE IVY

Traditional English carol

The holly and the ivy,
When they are both full grown,
Of all the trees that are in the wood,
The holly bears the crown.

Chorus

O, the rising of the sun,
And the running of the deer,
The playing of the merry organ,
Sweet singing in the choir.

The holly bears a blossom,
As white as lily flower,
And Mary bore sweet Jesus Christ,
To be our sweet Saviour.

Chorus

The holly bears a berry,
As red as any blood,
And Mary bore sweet Jesus Christ,
To do poor sinners good.

Chorus

The holly bears a prickle,
As sharp as any thorn,
And Mary bore sweet Jesus Christ,
On Christmas Day in the morn.

Chorus

The holly bears a bark,
As bitter as any gall,
And Mary bore sweet Jesus Christ,
For to redeem us all.

Chorus

EVERGREEN AND HOLLY

Written by E. O. Peck

Bring the evergreens and holly,
Bring the music and the song,
Chase away the melancholy,
By the pleasures bright, and jolly,
Which to Christmas time belong.

MISTLETOE

Written by Walter de la Mare

Sitting under the mistletoe
(Pale-green, fairy mistletoe),
One last candle burning low,
All the sleepy dancers gone,
Just one candle burning on,
Shadows lurking everywhere:
Someone came, and kissed me there.

Tired I was; my head would go
Nodding under the mistletoe
(Pale-green, fairy mistletoe),
No footsteps came, no voice, but only,
Just as I sat there, sleepy, lonely,
Stooped in the still and shadowy air
Lips unseen — and kissed me there.

CHRISTMAS GIFTS

THE NIGHT BEFORE CHRISTMAS

Written by Clement Clarke Moore

Twas the night before Christmas, when all through the house
Not a creature was stirring, not even a mouse.
The stockings were hung by the chimney with care,
In hopes that St Nicholas soon would be there.

The children were nestled all snug in their beds,
While visions of sugarplums danced in their heads.
And Mamma in her 'kerchief, and I in my cap,
Had just settled down for a long winter's nap.

When out on the lawn there arose such a clatter,
I sprang from the bed to see what was the matter.
Away to the window I flew like a flash,
Tore open the shutters and threw up the sash.

The moon on the breast of the new-fallen snow
Gave the lustre of midday to objects below.
When, what to my wondering eyes should appear,
But a miniature sleigh, and eight tiny reindeer.

With a little old driver, so lively and quick,
I knew in a moment it must be St Nick.
More rapid than eagles his coursers they came,
And he whistled, and shouted, and called them by name:

'Now, Dasher! Now, Dancer! Now, Prancer and Vixen!
On, Comet! On, Cupid! On, Donder and Blitzen!
To the top of the porch! To the top of the wall!
Now dash away! Dash away! Dash away all!'

As dry leaves that before the wild hurricane fly,
When they meet with an obstacle, mount to the sky;
So up to the housetop the coursers they flew,
With the sleigh full of toys, and St Nicholas too.

And then, in a twinkling, I heard on the roof
The prancing and pawing of each little hoof.
As I drew in my head, and was turning around,
Down the chimney St Nicholas came with a bound.

He was dressed all in fur, from his head to his foot,
And his clothes were all tarnished with ashes and soot.
A bundle of toys he had flung on his back,
And he looked like a peddler, just opening his pack.

His eyes, how they twinkled! His dimples, how merry!
His cheeks were like roses, his nose like a cherry!
His droll little mouth was drawn up like a bow,
And the beard on his chin was as white as the snow.

The stump of a pipe he held tight in his teeth,
And the smoke it encircled his head like a wreath.
He had a broad face and a little round belly,
That shook when he laughed, like a bowl full of jelly.

He was chubby and plump, a right jolly old elf,
And I laughed when I saw him, in spite of myself.
A wink of his eye and a twist of his head,
Soon gave me to know I had nothing to dread.

He spoke not a word, but went straight to his work,
And filled all the stockings, then turned with a jerk.
And laying his finger aside of his nose,
And giving a nod, up the chimney he rose.

He sprang to his sleigh, to his team gave a whistle,
And away they all flew like the down of a thistle.
But I heard him exclaim, 'ere he drove out of sight,
'Happy Christmas to all, and to all a good night!'

CHRISTMAS QUESTIONS

Written by Wolstan Dixey

How old is Santa Claus? Where does he keep?
And why does he come when I am asleep?
His hair is so white in the pictures I know,
Guess he stands on his head all the time in the snow.
But if he does that, then why don't he catch cold?
He must be as much as — most twenty years old.
I'd just like to see him once stand on his head,
And dive down the chimney, as grandmother said.
Why don't his head get all covered with black?
And if he comes head first, how can he get back?
Mamma knows about it, but she won't tell me.
I shall keep awake Christmas Eve, then I can see.
I have teased her to tell me, but Mamma she won't,
So I'll find out myself now; see if I don't.

WE THREE KINGS

Words by John Henry Hopkins

We three kings of Orient are,
Bearing gifts we traverse afar,
Field and fountain, moor and mountain,
Following yonder star.

Chorus

O Star of wonder, star of night,
Star with royal beauty bright,
Westward leading, still proceeding,
Guide us to thy perfect light.

Born a King on Bethlehem's plain,
Gold I bring to crown Him again,
King forever, ceasing never,
Over us all to reign.

Chorus

Frankincense to offer have I,
Incense owns a Deity nigh,
Prayer and praising, voices raising,
Worship Him, God most high.

Chorus

Myrrh is mine, its bitter perfume,
Breathes a life of gathering gloom,
Sorrowing, sighing, bleeding, dying,
Sealed in the stone-cold tomb.

Chorus

Glorious now behold Him arise,
King and God and sacrifice,
Heaven sings, 'Alleluia!'
'Alleluia!' the Earth replies.

Chorus

CHRISTMAS FOR THE LITTLE WOMEN

Adapted from Little Women, written by Louisa May Alcott

'Christmas won't be Christmas without any presents,' grumbled Jo, lying on the rug.

'It's so dreadful to be poor!' sighed Meg, looking down at her old dress.

'I don't think it's fair for some girls to have plenty of pretty things, and other girls nothing at all,' added little Amy, with an injured sniff.

'We've got Father and Mother, and each other,' said Beth contentedly from her corner.

The four young faces on which the firelight shone brightened at the cheerful words, but darkened again as Jo said sadly, 'We haven't got Father, and shall not have him for a long time.' She didn't say 'perhaps never', but each silently added it, thinking of Father far away, where the fighting was.

Nobody spoke for a minute, then Meg said in a different tone, 'You know the reason Mother suggested not having any presents this Christmas was because it is going to be a hard winter for everyone; and she thinks we shouldn't spend money for pleasure, when our men are suffering so in the army. We can't do much, but we can make our little sacrifices, and ought to do it gladly. But I am afraid I don't,' and Meg shook her head, as she thought regretfully of all the pretty things she wanted.

'I don't think the little we should spend would do any good. We've each got a dollar, and the army wouldn't be much helped by our giving that. I agree not to expect anything from Mother or you, but I do want to buy a novel for myself,' said Jo, who was a bookworm.

'I planned to spend mine on new music,' said Beth, with a little sigh, which no one heard but the hearth brush and kettle-holder.

'I shall get a nice box of Faber's drawing pencils; I really need them,' said Amy decidedly.

'Mother didn't say anything about our money, and she won't wish us to give up everything. Let's each buy what we want, and have a little fun. I'm sure we work hard enough to earn it,' cried Jo.

The clock struck six and, having swept up the hearth, Beth put a pair of slippers down to warm. Somehow the sight of the old shoes had a good effect upon the girls, for Mother was coming, and everyone brightened to welcome her. Meg stopped lecturing, and lit the lamp, Amy got out of the easy chair without being asked, and Jo forgot how tired she was as she sat up to hold the slippers nearer to the blaze.

'They are quite worn out. Marmee must have a new pair.'

'I thought I'd get her some with my dollar,' said Beth.

'No, I shall!' cried Amy.

'I'm the oldest,' began Meg.

But Jo cut in with a decided, 'I'm the man of the family now Papa is away, and I shall provide the slippers, for he told me to take special care of Mother while he was gone.'

'I'll tell you what we'll do,' said Beth, 'let's each get her something for Christmas, and not get anything for ourselves.'

'That's like you, dear!' exclaimed Jo. 'What will we get?'

Everyone thought for a minute, then Meg announced, as if the idea was suggested by the sight of her own pretty hands, 'I shall give her a nice pair of gloves.'

'Army shoes, best to be had,' cried Jo.

'Some handkerchiefs, all hemmed,' said Beth.

'I'll get a little bottle of cologne. She likes it, and it won't cost much, so I'll have some left to buy my pencils,' added Amy.

'How will we give the things?' asked Meg.

'Put them on the table, and bring her in and see her open the bundles. Don't you remember how we used to do on our birthdays?' answered Jo, and everyone agreed.

Jo was the first to wake in the grey dawn of Christmas morning. No stockings hung at the fireplace, and for a moment she felt disappointed as she remembered how, long ago, her little sock had fallen down because it was crammed so full of goodies. Then she remembered her mother had promised to leave something under her pillow. She slipped her hand under the pillow and drew out a little crimson-covered book. She woke Meg with a 'Merry Christmas,' and told her to see what was under her pillow. A green-covered book appeared, with a few words written by their mother, which made the present very precious in their eyes. Presently Beth and Amy woke to rummage and find their little books also – one dove-coloured; the other blue – and all sat looking at and talking about them, while the east grew rosy with the coming day.

'Where is Mother?' asked Meg, as she and Jo ran down to thank her for their gifts, half an hour later.

'Goodness only knows. Some poor creature came begging, and your ma went straight off to see what was needed,' replied Hannah, who had lived with the family since Meg was born, and was considered by them all more as a friend than a servant.

'She will be back soon, I think, so fry your cakes, and have everything ready,' said Meg, looking over the presents, which were collected in a basket ready to be produced at the proper time.

A bang on the street door sent the basket under the sofa, and the girls to the table, eager for breakfast.

'Merry Christmas, Marmee! Thank you for our books. We read some, and mean to every day,' they all cried in chorus.

'Merry Christmas, little daughters! I'm glad you began reading, and hope you will keep on. But I want to say one word before we sit down. Not far away from here lies a poor woman with a newborn baby. Six children are huddled into one bed to keep from freezing, for they have no fire. There is nothing to eat over there, and the oldest boy came to tell me they were suffering hunger and cold. My girls, will you give them your breakfast as a Christmas present?'

They were all unusually hungry, having waited nearly an hour, and for a minute no one spoke. But only for a minute, for Jo exclaimed suddenly, 'I'm so glad you came before we began!'

'May I help carry the things to the poor little children?' asked Beth eagerly.

'I shall take the cream and the muffins,' added Amy, heroically giving up the thing she most liked.

Meg was already piling the bread onto one big plate.

'I thought you'd do it,' said Mrs March, smiling as if satisfied. 'You shall all go and help me, and when we come back we will have bread and milk for breakfast, and make it up at dinnertime.'

They were soon ready, and the procession set out. Fortunately it was early, and they went through back streets, so few people saw them, and no one laughed at them.

A poor, bare, miserable room it was, with broken windows, no fire, ragged bedclothes, a sick mother, wailing baby and a group of pale, hungry children cuddled under one old quilt, trying to keep warm.

How the big eyes stared and the blue lips smiled as the girls went in.

'It is good angels come to us!' said the poor woman, crying for joy.

'Funny angels in hoods and mittens,' said Jo, and set them to laughing.

In a few minutes it really did seem as if kind spirits had been at work there. Hannah made a fire, and stopped up the broken panes with old hats and her own cloak. Mrs March gave the mother tea and porridge while she dressed the little baby as tenderly as if it had been her own. The girls meantime spread the table, set the children round the fire, and fed them like hungry birds, laughing and talking.

The children ate and warmed their purple hands at the comfortable blaze. And when the girls finally went away, leaving comfort behind, I think there were not in all the city four merrier people than the hungry little girls who gave away their breakfasts on Christmas morning.

'That's loving our neighbour better than ourselves, and I like it,' said Meg, as they set out their presents while their mother was upstairs collecting clothes for the poor family.

It was not a very splendid show, but there was a great deal of love in the few little bundles. The tall vase of red roses, white chrysanthemums and trailing vines, which stood in the middle, gave quite an elegant air to the table.

'She's coming! Open the door, Amy! Three cheers for Marmee!' cried Jo, prancing about while Meg went to conduct Mother to the seat of honour.

Beth played a happy march on the old piano, Amy threw open the door and Meg led their mother in with great dignity. Mrs March was both surprised and touched, and smiled with her eyes full as she examined her presents and read the little notes that accompanied them. The slippers went on at once, a new handkerchief was slipped into her pocket, well scented with Amy's cologne, a rose was pinned to her shirt and the nice gloves were pronounced a perfect fit.

There was a good deal of laughing and kissing and explaining, in the simple, loving fashion which makes these home festivals so pleasant at the time and so sweet to remember long afterward.

How Claus Made the First Toy

Adapted from a chapter of The Life and Adventures of Santa Claus, *written by L. Frank Baum*

Claus was left in the forest as a baby and was raised by the fairies and nymphs who found him. When he grew up, Claus left to find other humans. He walked through the valley and crossed the plain beyond to reach the people's houses, which stood alone or in groups of dwellings called villages. In nearly all the houses, whether big or little, there were children.

The youngsters soon came to know Claus's merry, laughing face and the kind glance of his bright eyes. The children played games with Claus. Wherever the young man chanced to be, the sound of childish laughter followed. You must know that in those days, children received little attention from their parents, so it was a marvel that Claus devoted his time to making them happy.

After a time, the winter drew near. The flowers lived out their lives, faded and disappeared; the beetles burrowed far into the warm earth; the butterflies deserted the meadows; and the voice of the brook grew hoarse, as if it had caught a cold.

One day, snowflakes fell and covered Claus's house in pure white. At night Jack Frost rapped at the door. 'Come in!' cried Claus.

'Come out!' answered Jack, 'for you have a fire inside.' So Claus came out. He had known Jack Frost in the forest, and liked the jolly rogue, though he mistrusted him.

'Isn't this glorious weather?' shouted the sprite. 'I shall nip scores of noses and ears and toes before daybreak.'

'If you love me, Jack, spare the children,' begged Claus. 'The young ones are weak, and cannot fight you.'

'True. Well, I will not pinch a child this night,' Jack promised sincerely. 'Goodnight, Claus!'

'Goodnight.' The young man went in and closed the door, and Jack Frost ran on to the nearest village.

Claus threw a log on the fire, which burned up brightly. Beside the hearth sat Blinkie, a big cat.

'I shall not see the children again soon,' said Claus to the cat. 'The snow will be deep for many days.'

The cat raised a paw and stroked her nose thoughtfully, but made no reply. So long as the fire burned and Claus sat in his easy chair by the hearth she did not mind the weather.

So passed many days and many long evenings. The cupboard was always full, but Claus became weary with having nothing to do but feed the fire from the big wood-pile.

One evening he picked up a stick of wood and began to cut it with his sharp knife. He had no thought, at first, except to occupy his time, and he whistled to the cat as he carved away portions of the stick. Puss sat up on her haunches and watched him.

Claus glanced at puss and then at the stick he was whittling, until presently the wood began to have a shape, and the shape was like the head of a cat.

Claus stopped whistling to laugh, and then both he and the cat looked at the wooden image in some surprise. Then he carved out the face, and rounded the lower part of the head so that it rested upon a neck.

Puss hardly knew what to make of it now, and sat up stiffly, as if watching with some suspicion what would come next.

Claus knew. He used his knife carefully, forming the body of the cat, which he made to sit upon its haunches as the real cat did, with her tail wound around her two front legs.

Finally Claus gave a loud and delighted laugh and placed the wooden cat, now completed, upon the hearth opposite the real cat.

Puss glared at her image, raised her hair in anger and uttered a defiant mew. The wooden cat paid no attention, and Claus, much amused, laughed again.

Then Blinkie advanced toward the wooden image to eye it closely and smell it. Eyes and nose told her the creature was wood, in spite of its natural appearance; so puss resumed her seat, but as she neatly washed her face with her padded paw she cast more than one admiring glance at her clever master.

The cat's master was pleased with his own handiwork, without knowing exactly why. Indeed, he had great cause to congratulate himself that night, and all the children throughout the world should have joined him rejoicing. For Claus had made his first toy.

CHRISTMAS AT GREEN GABLES

An excerpt from Anne of Green Gables, *written by Lucy Maud Montgomery*

Christmas morning broke on a beautiful white world. It had been a very mild December and people had looked forward to a green Christmas; but just enough snow fell softly in the night to transfigure Avonlea. Anne peeped out from her frosted gable window with delighted eyes. The firs in the Haunted Wood were all feathery and wonderful; the birches and wild cherry trees were outlined in pearl; the ploughed fields were stretches of snowy dimples; and there was a crisp tang in the air that was glorious. Anne ran downstairs singing until her voice re-echoed through Green Gables.

'Merry Christmas, Marilla! Merry Christmas, Matthew! Isn't it a lovely Christmas? I'm so glad it's white. Any other kind of Christmas doesn't seem real, does it? I don't like green Christmases. They're *not* green — they're just nasty faded browns and greys. What makes people call them green? Why — why — Matthew, is that for me? Oh, Matthew!'

Anne took the dress and looked at it in reverent silence. Oh, how pretty it was — a lovely soft brown gloria with all the gloss of silk; a skirt with dainty frills and shirrings; a waist elaborately pintucked in the most fashionable way, with a little ruffle of filmy lace at the neck. But the sleeves — they were the crowning glory! Long elbow cuffs, and above them two beautiful puffs divided by rows of shirring and bows of brown silk ribbon.

'That's a Christmas present for you, Anne,' said Matthew shyly. 'Why — why — Anne, don't you like it? Well now — well now.'

For Anne's eyes had suddenly filled with tears.

'*Like* it! Oh, Matthew!' Anne laid the dress over a chair and clasped her hands. 'Matthew, it's perfectly exquisite. Oh, I can never thank you enough. Look at those sleeves! Oh, it seems to me this must be a happy dream.'

'Well, well, let us have breakfast,' interrupted Marilla. 'I must say, Anne, I don't think you needed the dress; but since Matthew has got it for you, see that you take good care of it. There's a hair ribbon Mrs Lynde left for you. It's brown, to match the dress. Come now, sit in.'

'I don't see how I'm going to eat breakfast,' said Anne rapturously. 'Breakfast seems so commonplace at such an exciting moment. I'd rather feast my eyes on that dress. I'm so glad that puffed sleeves are still fashionable. It did seem to me that I'd never get over it if they went out before I had a dress with them. I'd never have felt quite satisfied, you see. It was lovely of Mrs Lynde to give me the ribbon too. I feel that I ought to be a very good girl indeed. It's at times like this I'm sorry I'm not a model little girl; and I always resolve that I will be in future. But somehow it's hard to carry out your resolutions when irresistible temptations come. Still, I really will make an extra effort after this.'

GOOD KING WENCESLAS

Words by John Mason Neale

Good King Wenceslas looked out,
On the feast of Stephen,
When the snow lay round about,
Deep and crisp and even.
Brightly shone the moon that night,
Though the frost was cruel,
When a poor man came in sight,
Gath'ring winter fuel.

'Hither, page, and stand by me,
If thou know'st it, telling,
Yonder peasant, who is he?
Where and what his dwelling?'
'Sire, he lives a good league hence,
Underneath the mountain,
Right against the forest fence,
By Saint Agnes' fountain.'

'Bring me food and bring me wine,
Bring me pine logs hither,
Thou and I will see him dine,
When we bear them thither.'
Page and monarch forth they went,
Forth they went together,
Through the cold wind's wild lament,
And the bitter weather.

'Sire, the night is darker now,
And the wind blows stronger,
Fails my heart, I know not how,
I can go no longer.'
'Mark my footsteps, my good page,
Tread thou in them boldly,
Thou shalt find the winter's rage,
Freeze thy blood less coldly.'

In his master's steps he trod,
Where the snow lay dinted,
Heat was in the very sod,
Which the Saint had printed.
Therefore, Christian men, be sure,
Wealth or rank possessing,
Ye who now will bless the poor,
Shall yourselves find blessing.

TWELVE DAYS OF CHRISTMAS

Traditional carol

On the first day of Christmas,
My true love sent to me
A partridge in a pear tree.

On the second day of Christmas,
My true love sent to me
Two turtle doves,
And a partridge in a pear tree.

On the third day of Christmas,
My true love sent to me
Three French hens,
Two turtle doves,
And a partridge in a pear tree.

On the fourth day of Christmas,
My true love sent to me
Four calling birds,
Three French hens,
Two turtle doves,
And a partridge in a pear tree.

On the fifth day of Christmas,
My true love sent to me
Five golden rings,
Four calling birds,
Three French hens,
Two turtle doves,
And a partridge in a pear tree.

On the sixth day of Christmas,
My true love sent to me
Six geese a-laying,
Five golden rings,
Four calling birds,
Three French hens,
Two turtle doves,
And a partridge in a pear tree.

On the seventh day of Christmas,
My true love sent to me
Seven swans a-swimming,
Six geese a-laying,
Five golden rings,
Four calling birds,
Three French hens,
Two turtle doves,
And a partridge in a pear tree.

On the eighth day of Christmas,
My true love sent to me
Eight maids a-milking,
Seven swans a-swimming,
Six geese a-laying,
Five golden rings,
Four calling birds,
Three French hens,
Two turtle doves,
And a partridge in a pear tree.

On the ninth day of Christmas,
My true love sent to me
Nine ladies dancing,
Eight maids a-milking,
Seven swans a-swimming,
Six geese a-laying,
Five golden rings,
Four calling birds,
Three French hens,
Two turtle doves,
And a partridge in a pear tree.

On the tenth day of Christmas,
My true love sent to me
Ten lords a-leaping,
Nine ladies dancing,
Eight maids a-milking,
Seven swans a-swimming,
Six geese a-laying,
Five golden rings,
Four calling birds,
Three French hens,
Two turtle doves,
And a partridge in a pear tree.

On the eleventh day of Christmas,
My true love sent to me
Eleven pipers piping,
Ten lords a-leaping,
Nine ladies dancing,
Eight maids a-milking,
Seven swans a-swimming,
Six geese a-laying,
Five golden rings,
Four calling birds,
Three French hens,
Two turtle doves,
And a partridge in a pear tree.

On the twelfth day of Christmas,
My true love sent to me
Twelve drummers drumming,
Eleven pipers piping,
Ten lords a-leaping,
Nine ladies dancing,
Eight maids a-milking,
Seven swans a-swimming,
Six geese a-laying,
Five golden rings,
Four calling birds,
Three French hens,
Two turtle doves,
And a partridge in a pear tree!

I SAW THREE SHIPS

Traditional English carol

I saw three ships come sailing in,
  On Christmas Day, on Christmas Day;
I saw three ships come sailing in,
On Christmas Day in the morning.

And what was in those ships all three,
On Christmas Day, on Christmas Day;
And what was in those ships all three,
On Christmas Day in the morning?

The Virgin Mary and Christ were there,
On Christmas Day, on Christmas Day;
The Virgin Mary and Christ were there,
On Christmas Day in the morning.

Pray, whither sailed those ships all three,
On Christmas Day, on Christmas Day;
Pray, whither sailed those ships all three,
On Christmas Day in the morning?

O they sailed into Bethlehem,
On Christmas Day, on Christmas Day;
O they sailed into Bethlehem,
On Christmas Day in the morning.

And all the bells on earth shall ring,
On Christmas Day, on Christmas Day;
And all the bells on earth shall ring,
On Christmas Day in the morning.

And all the angels in heaven shall sing,
On Christmas Day, on Christmas Day;
And all the angels in heaven shall sing,
On Christmas Day in the morning.

And all the souls on earth shall sing,
On Christmas Day, on Christmas Day;
And all the souls on earth shall sing,
On Christmas Day in the morning.

Then let us all rejoice again,
On Christmas Day, on Christmas Day;
Then let us all rejoice again,
On Christmas Day in the morning.

CHRISTMAS CHEER

SWEET HOME

Adapted from 'Dulce Domum' in The Wind in the Willows, *written by Kenneth Grahame*

Mole reached down a lantern from a nail on the wall and lit it, and the Rat, looking round him, saw that they were in a sort of forecourt. A garden seat stood on one side of the door, and on the other a roller; for the Mole, who was a tidy animal, could not stand having his ground kicked up by other animals into little runs that ended in earth heaps. On the walls hung wire baskets with ferns in them, alternating with brackets carrying plaster statues. Down on one side of the forecourt ran a skittle alley, with benches along it and little wooden tables. In the middle was a small round pond containing goldfish and surrounded by a cockle-shell border. Out of the centre of the pond rose a fanciful sculpture clothed in more cockle-shells and topped by a large silvered glass ball that reflected everything all wrong and had a very pleasing effect.

Mole's face beamed at the sight of all these objects so dear to him, and he hurried Rat through the door, lit a lamp, and took one glance round his old home. He saw the dust lying thick on everything, saw the cheerless, deserted look of the long-neglected house — and collapsed again on a hall chair, his nose to his paws. 'O Ratty!' he cried dismally, 'why ever did I do it? Why did I bring you to this poor, cold little place, when you might have been at River Bank, toasting your toes before a blazing fire, with all your own nice things about you!'

The Rat paid no heed. He was running here and there, opening doors and lighting lamps and candles. 'What a capital little house this is!' he called out cheerily. 'So compact! So well planned! We'll make a jolly night of it. The first thing we want is a good fire; I'll see to that. So this is the parlour? Splendid! Now, I'll fetch the wood and the coals, and you get a duster, Mole, and try and smarten things up a bit.'

Encouraged by his companion, the Mole roused himself and dusted and polished with energy, while the Rat soon had a cheerful blaze roaring up the chimney. He hailed the Mole to come and warm himself; but Mole had another fit of the blues, dropping down on a couch in dark despair and burying his face in his duster. 'Rat,' he moaned, 'how about your supper, you poor, cold, hungry, weary animal? I've nothing to give you – nothing – not a crumb!'

'What a fellow you are for giving in!' said the Rat reproachfully. 'Why, only just now I saw a sardine opener on the kitchen dresser; and everybody knows that means there are sardines about somewhere. Pull yourself together, and come with me and forage.'

They went hunting through every cupboard and turning out every drawer. The result was not so very depressing after all, though of course it might have been better: a tin of sardines, a box of captain's biscuits – nearly full – and a German sausage in silver paper.

'There's a banquet for you!' observed the Rat.

'No bread!' groaned the Mole; 'no butter, no—'

'No pâté de foie gras, no champagne!' continued the Rat, grinning. 'This is really the jolliest little place I ever was in. No wonder you're so fond of it, Mole. Tell us all about it, and how you came to make it what it is.'

While the Rat busied himself fetching plates, and knives and forks, the Mole related — somewhat shyly at first, but with more freedom as he warmed to his subject — how this was planned, and how that was thought out. Rat, who was desperately hungry but strove to conceal it, nodded seriously and said, 'wonderful', and 'most remarkable', at intervals, when the chance for an observation was given him.

At last the Rat had just got seriously to work with the sardine opener when sounds were heard from the forecourt — sounds like the scuffling of small feet in the gravel and a confused murmur of tiny voices — 'Now, all in a line — hold the lantern up a bit, Tommy — clear your throats first — no coughing after I say one, two, three. — Where's young Jane? — Here, come on, do, we're all a-waiting—'

'What's up?' inquired the Rat.

'I think it must be the fieldmice,' replied the Mole, with a touch of pride in his manner. 'They go round carol singing regularly at this time of the year. And they never pass me over. I used to give them hot drinks, and supper too sometimes, when I could afford it. It will be like old times to hear them again.'

'Let's have a look at them!' cried the Rat, jumping up and running to the door.

It was a pretty sight that met their eyes when they flung the door open. In the forecourt, lit by the dim rays of a lantern, some eight or ten little fieldmice stood in a semicircle, red comforters round their throats, their forepaws thrust deep into their pockets, their feet jigging for warmth. With bright beady eyes they glanced shyly at each other, sniggering a little, sniffing and applying coat sleeves a good deal.

As the door opened, one of the elder ones that carried the lantern was just saying, 'Now then, one, two, three!' and their shrill little voices uprose on the air, singing one of the old-time carols.

Villagers all, this frosty tide,
Let your doors swing open wide,
Though wind may follow, and snow beside,
Yet draw us in by your fire to bide;
Joy shall be yours in the morning!

Here we stand in the cold and the sleet,
Blowing fingers and stamping feet,
Come from far away you to greet —
You by the fire and we in the street —
Bidding you joy in the morning!

For ere one half of the night was gone,
Sudden a star has led us on,
Raining bliss and benison —
Bliss to-morrow and more anon,
Joy for every morning!

Goodman Joseph toiled through the snow —
Saw the star o'er a stable low;
Mary she might not further go —
Welcome thatch, and litter below!
Joy was hers in the morning!

And then they heard the angels tell
'Who were the first to cry NOEL?
Animals all, as it befell,
In the stable where they did dwell!
Joy shall be theirs in the morning!'

The voices ceased, the singers, bashful but smiling, exchanged sidelong glances, and silence succeeded – but for a moment only. Then, from up above and far away was borne to their ears in a faint musical hum the sound of distant bells ringing a joyful and clangorous peal.

'Very well sung, boys and girls!' cried the Rat heartily. 'And now come along in, all of you, and warm yourselves by the fire, and have something hot!'

'Yes, come along, fieldmice,' cried the Mole eagerly. 'This is quite like old times! Now, you just wait a minute, while we – O, Ratty!' he cried in despair. 'Whatever are we doing? We've nothing to give them!'

'You leave all that to me,' said the masterful Rat. 'Here, you with the lantern! I want to talk to you. Now, tell me, are there any shops open at this late hour?'

'Why, certainly, sir,' replied the fieldmouse respectfully. 'At this time of the year our shops keep open to all sorts of hours.'

'Then look here!' said the Rat. 'You go off at once, and you get me—'

Here much muttered conversation ensued, and the Mole only heard bits of it, such as – 'Fresh, mind! – no, a pound of that will do – no, only the best – if you can't get it there, try somewhere else – yes, of course, homemade, no tinned stuff – well then, do the best you can!' Finally, there was a clink of coin passing from paw to paw, the fieldmouse was provided with a basket, and off he hurried, he and his lantern.

The rest of the fieldmice, perched in a row on the settle, their small legs swinging, gave themselves up to enjoyment of the fire, and toasted their chilblains till they tingled; while the Mole, failing to draw them into easy conversation, made each of them recite the names of their numerous brothers, who were too young, it appeared, to be allowed to go out a-carolling this year.

The Rat, meanwhile, was busy examining the label on one of the bottles. 'Get the things ready, Mole,' he called out, 'while I draw the corks.'

It did not take long to prepare the brew, and soon every fieldmouse was sipping and coughing and choking and wiping his eyes and laughing and forgetting he had ever been cold in all his life.

'They act plays too, these fieldmice,' the Mole explained to the Rat. 'Make them up all by themselves. And very well they do it, too! They gave us a capital one last year, about a fieldmouse who was captured at sea and made to row in a galley; and when he escaped and got home again, his lady-love had gone into a convent. Here, YOU! You were in it, I remember. Get up and recite a bit.'

The fieldmouse addressed got up on his legs, giggled shyly, looked round the room, and remained absolutely tongue-tied. His comrades cheered him on, Mole coaxed and encouraged him, but nothing could overcome his stage fright. Then the latch clicked, the door opened and the fieldmouse with the lantern reappeared, staggering under the weight of his basket.

There was no more talk of play-acting once the contents of the basket had been tumbled out on the table. In a very few minutes supper was ready, and Mole, as he took the head of the table in a sort of a dream, saw his little friends' faces brighten and beam as they fell to without delay; and then let himself loose — for he was famished indeed — thinking what a happy homecoming this had turned out, after all. As they ate, they talked of old times, and the fieldmice gave him the local gossip, and answered as well as they could the hundred questions he had to ask them. The Rat said little or nothing, only taking care that each guest had what he wanted, and plenty of it, and that Mole had no trouble or anxiety about anything.

They clattered off at last, very grateful and showering wishes of the season, with their jacket pockets stuffed with remembrances for the small brothers and sisters at home. When the door had closed on the last of them and the chink of the lanterns had died away, Mole and Rat kicked the fire up, drew their chairs in and discussed the events of the long day. At last the Rat, with a tremendous yawn, said, 'Mole, old chap, I'm ready to drop. Sleepy is simply not the word. That your own bunk over on that side? Very well, then, I'll take this. What a ripping little house this is! Everything is so handy!'

He clambered into his bunk and rolled himself well up in the blankets, and slumber gathered him forthwith.

The weary Mole also was glad to turn in without delay, and soon had his head on his pillow, in great joy and contentment. But before he closed his eyes he let them wander round his old room, mellow in the glow of the firelight that played or rested on familiar and friendly things which had long been unconsciously a part of him, and now smilingly received him back. He was now in just the frame of mind that the tactful Rat had quietly worked to bring about in him. He saw clearly how plain and simple it all was; but clearly, too, how much it all meant to him.

HERE WE COME A-CAROLLING

Traditional English carol

Here we come a-carolling,
Among the leaves so green,
Here we come a-wand'ring,
So fair to be seen.

Chorus

Love and joy come to you,
And to you glad Christmas too,
And God bless you and send you,
A Happy New Year,
And God send you a Happy New Year.

We are not daily beggars,
That beg from door to door,
But we are neighbours' children,
Whom you have seen before.

Chorus

Bring us out a table,
And spread it with a cloth.
Bring us out a mouldy cheese,
And some of your Christmas loaf.

Chorus

God bless the master of this house,
Likewise the mistress too,
And all the little children,
That round the table go.

Chorus

Good master and good mistress,
While you're sitting by the fire,
Pray think of us poor children,
Who are wandering in the mire.

Chorus

A CHRISTMAS CAROL

Adapted from the story written by Charles Dickens

Marley was dead. There is no doubt about that. Scrooge and he were partners for many years. But Scrooge never painted out Old Marley's name. There it stood, years afterwards, above the warehouse door: Scrooge and Marley.

Hard and sharp as flint, the cold within Scrooge froze his old features, nipped his pointed nose, shrivelled his cheeks, made his eyes red and his thin lips blue. He carried his own low temperature about with him, and didn't thaw it one degree at Christmas.

One Christmas Eve, old Ebenezer Scrooge sat busy in his counting house. The door was open, so that Scrooge could keep his eye on his clerk, Bob Cratchit, who was copying letters.

'A merry Christmas, uncle!' cried a cheerful voice. It was Scrooge's nephew, Fred.

'Bah!' said Scrooge. 'Humbug!'

'Christmas a humbug, uncle!' said Fred. 'You don't mean that, I am sure?'

'I do,' said Scrooge. 'Merry Christmas! What right have you to be merry? You're poor enough.'

'What right have you to be dismal?' returned Fred gaily, 'You're rich enough.'

Scrooge said, 'Bah!' again, and followed it up with 'Humbug!'

'Don't be angry, uncle. Come! Dine with us tomorrow.'

Scrooge refused and his nephew left.

At the end of the day, Bob Cratchit snuffed his candle out and put on his hat.

'You'll want all day off tomorrow, I suppose?' said Scrooge.

'If it's convenient, sir,' said Bob.

'I suppose you must have the whole day. But be here all the earlier next morning.'

The clerk promised that he would, and Scrooge walked out with a growl.

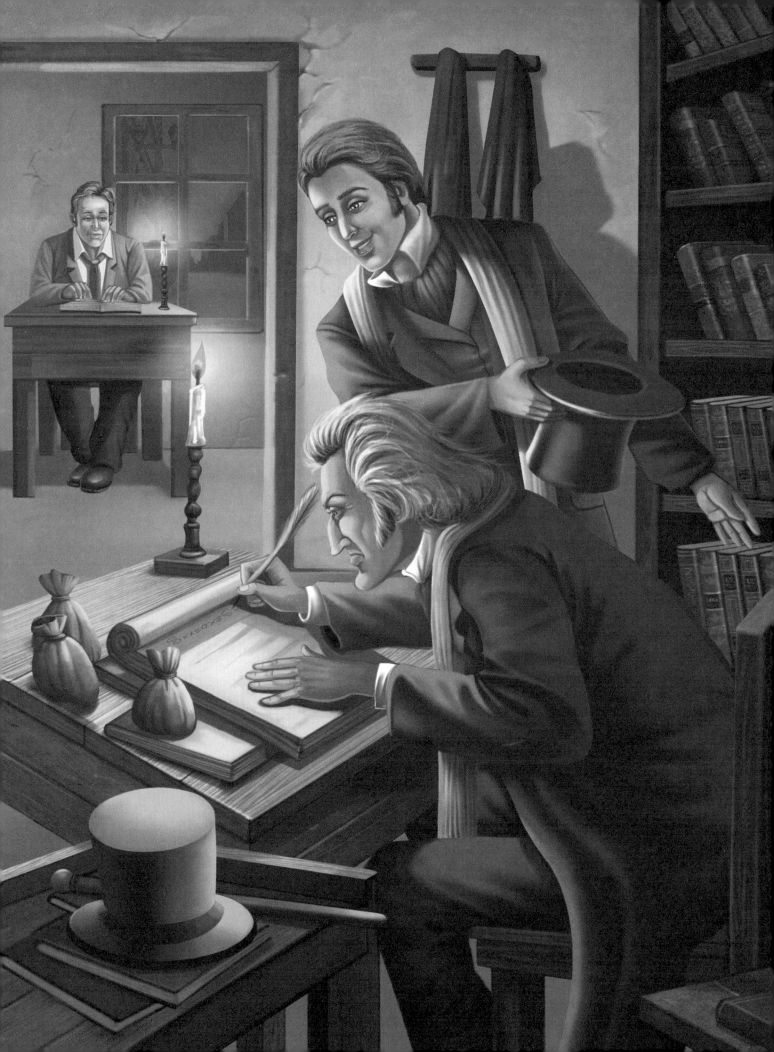

Scrooge went home. The yard was dark as he put his key in the lock. Strangely, he saw the face of his dead partner, Marley, in the door knocker. Then all of a sudden the face was gone.

He paused for a moment before he shut the door, and looked cautiously behind it, but seeing nothing unusual, he closed it with a bang.

'Humbug!' said Scrooge as he walked through the house and prepared for bed. He sat down and his glance happened to rest upon a bell that hung in the room. As he looked, he saw the bell begin to swing. Soon it rang out loudly, and so did every bell in the house.

All of a sudden, the bells ceased, and there was a clanking noise, as if someone were dragging a heavy chain in the cellar. The cellar door flew open with a booming sound, and Scrooge heard the noise coming up the stairs, then straight towards his door.

'It's humbug still!' said Scrooge. 'I won't believe it.'

His colour changed, though, when a transparent figure came through the heavy door, and passed into the room before his eyes.

Scrooge, sharp and cold as ever, said, 'Who are you?'

'Ask me who I *was*.'

'Who *were* you, then?' said Scrooge, raising his voice.

'In life I was your partner, Jacob Marley. You don't believe in me,' observed the Ghost.

'I don't,' said Scrooge.

At this the spirit raised a frightful cry, and shook its chain with such an appalling noise, that Scrooge held on tight to his chair.

'You are chained,' said Scrooge, trembling. 'Tell me why?'

'I wear the chain I forged in life by being greedy and doing wrong to others,' replied the Ghost. 'I am here tonight to warn you that you have yet a chance and hope of escaping my fate, Ebenezer. You will be haunted by Three Spirits.'

'I – I think I'd rather not,' said Scrooge.

'Without their visits,' said the Ghost, 'you cannot hope to shun the path I tread. Expect the first when the bell tolls one.'

The spectre floated out into the bleak, dark night. Scrooge closed the window and examined the door by which the Ghost had entered. He tried to say 'Humbug!' but stopped at the first syllable. He went straight to bed without undressing, and fell asleep instantly.

When Scrooge awoke it was dark. He listened for the hour. It chimed twelve! Scrooge remembered that Marley's Ghost had warned him of a visitation when the bell tolled one. He decided to lie awake until the hour passed.

When the hour bell sounded, the curtains of his bed were drawn aside by a hand. Scrooge saw a strange figure – like a child, yet also like an old man. It wore a tunic of the purest white. It held a branch of fresh green holly. From the crown of its head there sprung a bright clear jet of light.

'Are you the Spirit, sir, whose coming was foretold to me?' asked Scrooge.

'I am!'

The voice was soft and gentle.

'Who and what are you?' Scrooge demanded.

'I am the Ghost of Christmas Past.'

It put out its strong hand as it spoke, and clasped him gently by the arm.

'Rise and walk with me!'

He rose, and they passed through the wall and onto an open country road. The city had vanished.

'Good Heaven!' said Scrooge as he looked about. 'I was a boy here!'

As they walked along the road some boys went by. They were in great spirits and shouted to each other.

'These are but shadows of the things that have been,' said the Ghost. 'They cannot see us.'

As the travellers came, Scrooge knew every one. Why did his heart leap up as they went past? Why was he filled with gladness when he heard them say 'Merry Christmas'? What was merry Christmas to Scrooge?

'The school is not quite deserted,' said the Ghost. 'A solitary child, neglected by his friends, is left there still.'

Scrooge said he knew it and he sobbed.

They left the road and approached the school. In a bare, melancholy room sat a lonely boy reading at a desk. Scrooge sat down and wept, because the poor forgotten boy was himself as a child.

The Ghost waved its hand, saying as it did so, 'Let us see another Christmas!'

They left the school behind them and were now in a busy city. It was Christmas time again.

The Ghost stopped at a warehouse door, and asked Scrooge if he knew it.

'Know it!' said Scrooge. 'Was I apprenticed here?'

They went in. There was an old gentleman in a wig, sitting behind a high desk. Scrooge cried in great excitement, 'Why, it's old Fezziwig! Bless his heart, it's Fezziwig alive again!'

Old Fezziwig laid down his pen, and called out, in a jovial voice, 'Yo ho, there, Ebenezer!'

Scrooge's former self, now grown a young man, came briskly in.

'No more work tonight. Christmas Eve, Ebenezer!'

In came a fiddler and in came Mrs Fezziwig, smiling. In came all the young men and women employed in the business.

There were dances, and there was cake, and there were mince pies.

When the clock struck eleven, the ball broke up. Mr and Mrs Fezziwig stood on either side the door, shook hands with every person and wished them all a merry Christmas.

Scrooge's heart and soul were in the scene, and with his former self. He remembered everything, and enjoyed everything.

Scrooge felt the Spirit's glance, and stopped.

'What is the matter?' asked the Ghost.

'Nothing,' said Scrooge.

'Something, I think?' the Ghost insisted.

'I should like to be able to say a word or two to my clerk Bob Cratchit just now. That's all.'

'My time grows short,' observed the Spirit. 'Quick!'

Again Scrooge saw himself. He was older now. He was not alone, but sat by the side of a fair young girl in whose eyes there were tears.

'It matters little,' she said softly. 'Money is more important to you than I am. If it can cheer and comfort you in time to come, I have no cause to grieve. I can't marry you, Ebenezer.'

'Spirit!' said Scrooge in a broken voice, 'remove me from this place. I cannot bear it! Take me back! Haunt me no longer!'

Scrooge was exhausted and overcome with drowsiness. He realised he was in his own bedroom. He barely had time to stagger to bed before he sank into a heavy sleep.

After waking, Scrooge waited for the second messenger. But, when no shape appeared, he was taken with a violent fit of trembling. At last, he got up softly, and shuffled in his slippers to the door.

The moment Scrooge's hand was on the lock, a strange voice called his name.

'Come in!' exclaimed the Ghost. 'Come in and know me better, man!'

Scrooge entered timidly, and hung his head before this Spirit.

'I am the Ghost of Christmas Present,' said the Spirit. 'Look upon me!'

Scrooge did so. It was clothed in one simple deep green robe, bordered with white fur. Its feet were bare and on its head it wore a holly wreath. Its dark brown curls were long and free. It had a friendly face, sparkling eyes and a cheery voice.

'Touch my robe!' said the Spirit.

Scrooge did as he was told, and held the robe tightly. The room vanished and they stood in the city streets on Christmas morning. The people were jovial and full of glee. The Spirit took Scrooge to Bob Cratchit's house.

Mrs Cratchit was preparing Christmas dinner. The older children helped while the younger Cratchits danced about the table. In came Bob with Tiny Tim upon his shoulder. Tiny Tim carried a little crutch, and had iron frames on his legs.

The Cratchits' Christmas dinner was a small one for a large family, but they were happy, grateful, pleased with one another and contented. After dinner Bob proposed a toast: 'A merry Christmas to us all, my dears. God bless us!'
The family echoed his toast.

'God bless us every one!' said Tiny Tim, the last of all. He sat very close to his father's side. Bob held Tim's little hand in his.

'Spirit,' said Scrooge with an interest he had never felt before, 'tell me if Tiny Tim will live.'

'I see a vacant seat,' replied the Ghost, 'and a crutch without an owner.'

'No, no,' said Scrooge. 'Oh, no, kind Spirit! Say he will be spared.'

Scrooge was overcome grief.

As the family faded, Scrooge kept his eye upon them, and especially on Tiny Tim, until the last.

It was a great surprise to Scrooge to hear a hearty laugh and to suddenly find himself in a bright, gleaming room, with the Spirit standing smiling by his side.

'Ha, ha!' laughed Scrooge's nephew, Fred. 'Ha, ha, ha!' Fred's wife and their guests laughed too.

'He said that Christmas was a humbug, as I live!' cried Fred. 'He believed it, too! He's a comical old fellow and not so pleasant as he might be, but I have nothing to say against him.'

'I have no patience with him,' said Fred's wife.

'Oh, I have!' said Scrooge's nephew. 'I am sorry for him; I couldn't be angry with him if I tried. Who suffers by his ill whims? Himself always. A merry Christmas and a happy New Year to the old man, whatever he is!'

Scrooge felt so lighthearted that he would have thanked Fred if the Ghost had given him time. But the whole scene disappeared.

Scrooge looked for the Ghost, but it was gone. Instead, he saw a new Phantom, draped and hooded, coming like a mist along the ground towards him. The Phantom was shrouded in a deep black garment, which left nothing of it visible, except one outstretched hand. The Spirit did not speak.

'I am in the presence of the Ghost of Christmas Yet to Come?' said Scrooge.

The Spirit did not answer, but pointed onward with its hand.

'You are about to show me shadows of the things that have not happened?'

The Spirit seemed to nod its head slightly.

'Ghost of the Future!' exclaimed Scrooge, 'I fear you more than any spectre I have seen. But, as I hope to live to be a different man than I was, I am prepared to bear you company. Will you not speak to me?'

It gave him no reply. The hand was pointed straight before them.

'Lead on, Spirit!' said Scrooge.

The phantom moved away and Scrooge followed.

The Spirit stopped beside a little knot of businessmen. Scrooge listened to them.

'I don't know much about it. I only know he's dead,' said one.

'What has he done with his money?' asked another.

'I haven't heard,' said the first man. 'He hasn't left it to *me*. That's all I know.'

This pleasantry was received with a general laugh.

The Phantom glided on. The scene changed, and Scrooge saw a bare, uncurtained bed, on which there lay the covered body of a man – all alone, with no one to weep for him.

The Spirit continued on and Scrooge joined it in a churchyard. The Spirit stood among the graves, and pointed to one.

Scrooge crept towards it, trembling as he went and, following the finger, read upon the stone of the neglected grave his own name, EBENEZER SCROOGE.

'Am *I* that man who lay upon the bed?' he cried.

The finger pointed from the grave to him, and back again.

'No, Spirit! Oh no, no!' said Scrooge, 'May I yet change these shadows you have shown me?'

The hand trembled.

'I will honour Christmas in my heart, and try to keep it all the year. Oh, tell me I may wipe away the writing on this stone!'

Holding up his hands in a last prayer to have his fate reversed, he saw the Phantom's hood and dress shrink and then collapse.

Scrooge was back in his own bed in his own room. Best and happiest of all, there was still time to make amends!

Scrooge was laughing and crying at once. 'I am as light as a feather, I am as happy as an angel, I am as merry as a schoolboy. A merry Christmas to everybody! A happy New Year to all the world!'

Running to the window, he opened it and put out his head. 'What's today?' cried Scrooge, calling down to a boy below.

'Today!' replied the boy. 'Why, CHRISTMAS DAY.'

'It's Christmas Day!' said Scrooge. 'I haven't missed it. Do you know the shop in the next street? Have they sold the prize turkey that was hanging up there? The big one?'

'What – the one as big as me?' returned the boy. 'It's hanging there now.'

'Is it?' said Scrooge. 'Go and buy it. Come back with it in less than five minutes, and I'll give you half a crown!'

The boy was off like a shot.

'I'll send it to Bob Cratchit's,' whispered Scrooge with a laugh. 'It's twice the size of Tiny Tim!' He wrote out the address with a shaking hand, paid for the turkey when it arrrived and sent it to Bob Cratchit's, chuckling all the while.

Scrooge dressed himself in his best and went out. He gave each person passing by a delighted smile.

He went to his nephew's house for dinner. Fred was so glad to see his uncle it is a mercy he didn't shake his arm off. Scrooge felt at home in five minutes and enjoyed a wonderful Christmas party!

Scrooge was early at the office next morning. Bob Cratchit was late. Scrooge sat with his door wide open.

'Hallo!' growled Scrooge in his usual voice. 'What do you mean by coming here at this time of day?'

'I am very sorry, sir,' said Bob.

'Step this way, sir, if you please,' said Scrooge.

'It's only once a year, sir,' pleaded Bob. 'It shall not be repeated.'

'Now, I'll tell you what, my friend,' said Scrooge. 'I am not going to stand this sort of thing any longer. And therefore,' he continued, 'I am about to raise your salary! A merry Christmas, Bob!' said Scrooge earnestly. 'A merrier Christmas, Bob, than I have given you for many a year! I'll raise your salary, and try to help your struggling family.'

Scrooge was better than his word. He did it all, and infinitely more; and to Tiny Tim, who did NOT die, he was a second father. He became as good a friend, as good a master and as good a man as the good old city knew.

It was always said of him afterwards that he knew how to keep Christmas well. May that be truly said of all of us! And so, as Tiny Tim observed, God bless us, every one!

WE WISH YOU A MERRY CHRISTMAS

Traditional carol

We wish you a merry Christmas,
We wish you a merry Christmas,
We wish you a merry Christmas,
And a happy New Year!

Chorus
Good tidings we bring to you
and your kin;
We wish you a merry Christmas
and a happy New Year.

Now bring us some figgy pudding,
Now bring us some figgy pudding,
Now bring us some figgy pudding,
And bring some out here.

Chorus

For we all like figgy pudding,
For we all like figgy pudding,
For we all like figgy pudding,
So bring some out here.

Chorus
And we won't go until we've got some,
And we won't go until we've got some,
And we won't go until we've got some,
So bring some out here.

Chorus

CHRISTMAS
AROUND THE
WORLD

A Story of the Christ Child

Adapted from Elizabeth Harrison's retelling of a German legend

Once upon a time, on the night before Christmas, a little child wandered all alone through the streets of a great city. There were many people hurrying home with bundles of presents for each other and for their little ones. Fine carriages rolled by and all things seemed in a hurry and glad about the coming Christmas morning.

From some of the windows bright lights were beginning to stream. But the little child seemed to have no home. No one took any notice of him except perhaps Jack Frost, who bit his bare toes and made the ends of his fingers tingle. The north wind, too, seemed to notice the child, for it blew against him and pierced his ragged clothes, causing him to shiver. Home after home he passed, looking with longing eyes through the windows in upon happy children, most of whom were helping to trim Christmas trees for the next day.

'Surely,' said the child to himself, 'where there is so much happiness, some of it may be for me.' So with timid steps he approached a large house. Through the windows, he could see a tall and stately Christmas tree already lighted. Many presents hung upon it. Its green boughs were trimmed with gold and silver ornaments. Slowly he climbed up the broad steps and gently rapped at the door.

It was opened by a servant. He had a kindly face, although his voice was deep and gruff. He looked at the little child for a moment, then sadly shook his head and said, 'Go down off the steps. There is no room here for you.' He looked sorry as he spoke, but the child had to turn back into the cold and darkness.

The street grew colder and darker. The child went sadly forward, saying to himself, 'Is there no one in this great city who will share Christmas with me?' Farther down the street he wandered, to where the homes were not so large. There seemed to be little children inside nearly all the houses. Christmas trees could be seen in nearly every window, with beautiful dolls and trumpets and picture books and balls and other toys hung upon them. In one window the child noticed a little lamb made of soft white wool. It had been hung on the tree for one of the children. The little stranger stopped before this window and looked at the beautiful things inside, but most of all was he drawn to the white lamb. At last, creeping up to the windowpane, he gently tapped upon it.

A little girl came to the window and looked out into the dark street where the snow had now begun to fall. She saw the child, but she only frowned and shook her head. Back into the dark, cold streets the child turned again.

Again and again the little child rapped softly at door or windowpane. At each place he was refused. The hours passed; later grew the night, and colder grew the wind, and darker seemed the street. Farther and farther the little one wandered. There was scarcely anyone left upon the street by this time. Suddenly, ahead of him, there appeared a bright, single ray of light. It shone through the darkness into the child's eyes. He looked up smilingly and said, 'I will go where the small light beckons, perhaps they will share their Christmas with me.'

Hurrying past the other houses, he soon reached the end of the street and went straight up to the window from which the light was streaming. It was a small, plain house. The light seemed to call him in. From what do you suppose the light came? Nothing but a candle, which had been placed in an old cup in the window, as a glad token of Christmas Eve. There were no curtains or shades on the small window, and as the little child looked in he saw a Christmas tree branch standing upon a neat wooden table. The room was plainly furnished, but it was very clean. Near the fireplace sat a mother with a little child on her knee and an older child beside her. The two children were listening to their mother tell a story. She must have been telling them a Christmas story, I think. A few bright coals were burning in the fireplace, and all seemed warm.

The little wanderer crept closer. So sweet was the mother's face, so loving seemed the children, that at last he took courage and tapped very gently on the door. The mother stopped talking, the children looked up. 'What was that, mother?' asked the girl.

'I think it was someone tapping on the door. Run quickly and open it. No one must be left out in the cold on our beautiful Christmas Eve.'

The child ran to the door and threw it open. The mother saw the ragged stranger, cold and shivering. She held out both hands and drew him into the warm room. 'You poor, dear child,' she said, putting her arms around him. 'He is very cold, my children,' she exclaimed. 'We must warm him.'

'And,' added the girl, 'we must love him and give him some of our Christmas.'

The mother sat down by the fire with the little child on her lap, and her own little ones warmed his half-frozen hands in theirs. The mother smoothed his tangled curls, and kissed the child's face. She gathered the three little ones in her arms. For a moment the room was very still. The girl said softly to her mother, 'May we light the Christmas tree, and let him see how beautiful it looks?'

'Yes,' said the mother. With that she sat the child beside the fire, and went herself to fetch the few simple ornaments which from year to year she had saved for her children's Christmas tree. They were soon so busy that they did not notice the room had filled with a strange and brilliant light. They turned and looked at the spot where the little wanderer sat. His ragged clothes had changed to garments white and beautiful; his curls seemed like a halo of golden light about his head; but most glorious of all was his face, which shone with a light so dazzling that they could scarcely look upon it.

In silent wonder they gazed at the child. Their little room seemed to grow larger and larger, until the roof of their house seemed to expand and rise, until it reached to the sky.

With a sweet and gentle smile the wonderful child looked upon them for a moment, and then slowly rose and floated through the air, above the treetops, beyond the church spire, higher even than the clouds themselves, until he appeared to them to be a shining star in the sky above. At last he disappeared from sight. The astonished children turned in hushed awe to their mother, and said in a whisper, 'Oh, mother, it was the Christ Child, was it not?' And the mother answered in a low tone, 'Yes.'

And it is said, dear children, that each Christmas Eve the little Christ Child wanders through some town or village, and those who receive him and take him into their homes and hearts are given this marvellous vision.

THE LEGEND OF THE POINSETTIA

Adapted from a Mexican legend

A long time ago in a village in Mexico, there lived a little girl called Maria and her younger brother Pablo. Although their family was very poor, the children were generous and kind-hearted.

Maria and Pablo took great joy in celebrating Christmas, even though their family could not afford many gifts. They looked forward to the Christmas festival in their village all year long, and they especially loved the nativity display at their church. The local children liked to bring gifts to the manger for the baby Jesus. Maria and Pablo dearly wanted to bring a special gift like the other children, but they had no money to buy one.

On Christmas Eve, *la Noche Buena*, Maria and Pablo walked slowly and sadly to the church. On their way they looked for some wild flowers to bring, but they found only weeds. The children began to cry. Suddenly, an angel appeared in the darkness. At first the children were frightened, but the angel spoke softly and told them not to cry. The angel told the children to pick the weeds and take them to the church. Then the angel disappeared.

Amazed, the two children picked the weeds and eagerly carried them to the church. They strode bravely into the village, while the other children laughed and teased them for bringing weeds as a gift. Ignoring the taunts of the other children, Maria and Pablo approached the nativity display and placed the weeds gently around the manger of the baby Jesus.

Miraculously, scarlet star-shaped flowers grew from the weeds. Overjoyed, Maria and Pablo realised they had given the most beautiful gift of all.

Today, those flowers are known as poinsettias. People in Mexico and other places around the world use poinsettias as Christmas decorations.

BABUSHKA

A Russian legend, adapted from Twilight Stories, author unknown

If you were a Russian child you would not watch to see Santa Claus coming down the chimney. Instead you would stand by the window to catch a peep at poor Babushka as she hurries by.

Who is Babushka? Is she Santa Claus's wife?

No, indeed. She is only a poor little crooked wrinkled old woman, who comes at Christmas time into everybody's house, who peeps into every cradle, drops a tear on the baby's white pillow, and goes away feeling very, very sorrowful.

And not only at Christmas time, but also throughout the cold winter, and in March, when the wind blows loud, and whistles and howls and dies away like a sigh, the Russian children hear the rustling step of the Babushka. She is always in a hurry. One hears her running fast along the crowded streets and over the quiet country fields. She seems to be out of breath and tired, yet she hurries on.

She scarcely looks at the little children as they press their rosy faces against the windowpane and whisper to each other, 'Will the Babushka visit us?'

No, she will not stop. Only on Christmas Eve will she come upstairs into the nursery and give each little one a present. You must not think she leaves handsome gifts such as Santa Claus brings for you. She does not bring bicycles or dolls. She does not come in a little sleigh drawn by reindeer, but hobbling along on foot, and she leans on a crutch. She has her old apron filled with candy and cheap toys, and the children all love her dearly. They watch to see her come, and when one hears a rustling, he cries, 'The Babushka!' Then all the others look, but they must turn their heads very quickly or she vanishes. I never saw her myself.

Best of all, she loves little babies and, often, when the tired mothers sleep, she bends over their cradles and looks very carefully.

What is she looking for?

Ah, that you can't guess unless you know her sad story.

Long, long ago, the Babushka, who was even then an old woman, was busy sweeping her little hut. She lived alone in the coldest corner of cold Russia, in a lonely place where four wide roads met. These roads were white with snow, for it was wintertime. In the summer, when the fields were full of flowers and the air full of sunshine and singing birds, Babushka's home did not seem so very quiet; but in the winter, with only the snowflakes and the shy snow birds and the loud wind for company, the little old woman felt very cheerless. But she was a busy old woman and, as it was already twilight and her home but half swept, she felt in a great hurry to finish her work before bedtime.

Presently, down the widest and the loneliest of the white roads, there appeared a long train of people. They were moving slowly. As the procession came nearer, Babushka was frightened at the splendour. There were Three Kings with crowns on their heads. Their long cloaks protected them from the freezing cold, and they rode camels whose hooves left strange tracks in the snow.

Servants carried heavy loads on their backs, and each King carried a present. One carried a beautiful bowl, and in the fading light Babushka could see in it a golden liquid, which she knew from its colour must be myrrh. Another held a decorated box, and it seemed to be heavy, as indeed it was, for it was full of gold. The third carried a vase and from the rich perfume that filled the snowy air, one could guess the vase was filled with frankincense.

Babushka was terribly frightened, so she hid in her hut. The servants knocked a long time before Babushka opened the door. They asked which road they should take to a faraway town. Babushka knew the way across the fields to the nearest village, but she knew nothing else of the wide world. The servants scolded, but the Three Kings spoke kindly to her, and asked her to show them the way as far as she knew it. They told her they had seen a Star in the sky and were following it to a little town where a Child lay. They had lost sight of the Star because of the falling snow.

'Who is the Child?' asked the old woman.

'He is a King, and we go to worship him,' they answered. 'These presents of gold, frankincense and myrrh are for Him. Come with us, Babushka!'

The woman shook her head. No, she wanted to put her hut in order – perhaps she would be ready to go tomorrow. But the Three Kings could not wait; so when the sun rose they were gone. It seemed like a dream to poor Babushka, for even the camels' tracks were covered by the deep white snow.

Now that the sun was shining, she wished she had gone with the travellers. She thought a great deal about the dear Baby that the Three Kings had gone to worship, for she had no children of her own. The more she brooded on the thought, the more miserable she grew.

After a while the Child became her first thought at waking and her last at night. One day she shut the door of her house forever, and set out on a long journey.

Babushka longed to find the Child, that she too might love and worship Him. She asked everyone she met, and some people thought her crazy, but others gave her kind answers.

People told Babushka how He was born in a manger, and many other things. The old woman had but one idea in her head. The Three Kings had gone to seek the Christ Child. She would, if not too late, seek Him too.

She forgot, I am sure, how many long years had gone by. She looked in vain for the baby in His manger-cradle. She spent all her little savings on toys and candy to make friends with little children so that they might not run away when she came hobbling into their nurseries.

Now you know for whom she is sadly seeking when she bends down over each baby's pillow. Sometimes, when the old grandmother sits nodding by the fire, and the bigger children sleep in their beds, old Babushka comes hobbling into the room, and whispers softly, 'Is the young Child here?'

Ah, no. She has come too late, too late. But the little children know her and love her. Two thousand years ago she lost the chance of finding Him. Crooked, wrinkled, old, sick and sorry, she yet lives on, looking into each baby's face – always disappointed, always seeking. Will she find Him at last?

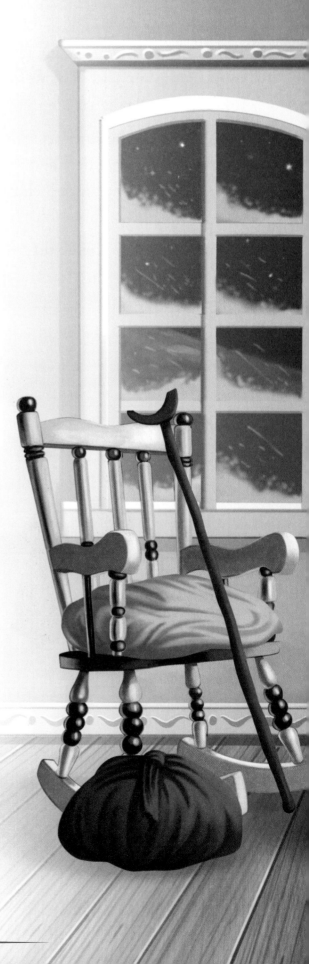

THE VIRGIN MARY HAD A BABY BOY

Traditional West Indian carol

The Virgin Mary had a baby boy,
The Virgin Mary had a baby boy,
The Virgin Mary had a baby boy,
And they say that His name was Jesus.

Chorus

He come from the glory,
He come from the glorious kingdom.
He come from the glory,
He come from the glorious kingdom.
Oh yes, believer! Oh yes, believer!
He come from the glory,
He come from the glorious kingdom.

The angels sang when the baby born,
The angels sang when the baby born,
The angels sang when the baby born,
And proclaimed Him the Saviour Jesus.

Chorus

The shepherds came where the baby born,
The shepherds came where the baby born,
The shepherds came where the baby born,
And they say that His name was Jesus.

Chorus

The Wise Men saw where the baby born,
The Wise Men saw where the baby born,
The Wise Men saw where the baby born,
And they say that His name was Jesus.

Chorus

GOOD NEWS FOR EVERYONE

Traditional Zambian carol

Chorus

Here's good news for everyone: great happiness is ours!
Rejoice and be glad for the Saviour has come to the earth from God.

With wondrous love despite our sin,
God sought our faithless hearts to win.

Chorus

PICCOLA

Adapted from the story written by Nora A. Smith

Piccola and her mother lived in Italy in an old stone house that looked onto a dark, narrow street. They were very poor, and the mother was often away from home, washing clothes and scrubbing floors to earn money for her little girl and herself. Piccola was alone a great deal of the time. She had no playthings except a heap of stones in the backyard and a very old, very ragged doll.

But there was a small round hole in the stone wall at the back of the yard, and Piccola's greatest pleasure was to look through that into her neighbour's garden. When she put her eyes to the hole, she could see the green grass and smell the sweet flowers. She had never seen anyone walking in the garden, for it belonged to an old gentleman who did not care about grass and flowers.

One day Piccola's mother told her that the old gentleman had gone away, and had rented his house to an American family. After this, Piccola was never lonely, for all day long she watched the children playing in the garden. One day they saw Piccola's black eyes looking through the hole in the stones. They were a little frightened at first; but the next day Rose, the oldest girl, talked to her a little. When the children found that she had no one to play with, they talked to her every day through the hole in the wall.

The little boy said he would ask his father to make the hole larger, and then Piccola could come and play with them. The father had some of the stones broken away and an opening made for Piccola to come in.

How excited she was, and how glad the children were when she stepped into the garden! She wore her best dress and favourite shoes, but no stockings because Piccola and her mother had no money to buy any. What a good time the children had that day!

December came and the little Americans began to talk about Christmas. One day, they all asked her what she thought she would have for a Christmas present. 'A Christmas present!' said Piccola. 'Why, what is that?'

All the children looked surprised at this, and Rose said, rather gravely, 'Dear Piccola, don't you know what Christmas is?'

Oh, yes, Piccola knew it was a happy day, but what was a Christmas present?

Then the children began to laugh and to answer her all together. There was such a clatter that she could hear only a few words, such as 'chimney', 'Santa Claus', 'stockings', 'reindeer', 'Christmas Eve' and 'toys'. Piccola put her hands over her ears and said, 'Oh, I can't understand one word. You tell me, Rose.'

So Rose told her all about jolly Santa Claus, with his red cheeks and white beard and fur coat, and about his reindeer and sleigh full of toys. 'Every Christmas Eve,' said Rose, 'he comes down the chimney, and fills the stockings of all good children; so, Piccola, you hang up your stocking, and who knows what a beautiful Christmas present you will find when morning comes!'

Later Piccola told her mother about Santa Claus, and her mother seemed to think that perhaps he did not know there was any little girl in their house. But Piccola felt very sure Santa Claus would remember her, for her little friends had promised to send a letter up the chimney to remind him.

Christmas Eve came at last. Piccola's mother hurried home from her work. They had their supper and soon it was bedtime – time to get ready for Santa Claus. But Piccola remembered then for the first time that the children had told her she must hang up her stocking, and she hadn't any, and neither had her mother.

How sad it was! Now Santa Claus would come, and perhaps be angry because he couldn't find any place to put the present.

The poor little girl stood by the fireplace, and the big tears began to run down her cheeks. Just then her mother called to her, 'Hurry, Piccola; come to bed.' What should she do? But she stopped crying, and tried to think; and in a moment she remembered her shoes, and ran off to get one of them. She put it close to the chimney, and said to herself, 'Surely Santa Claus will know what it's there for. He will know I haven't any stockings, so I gave him the shoe instead.'

Then she went off happily to her bed.

The sun had only just begun to shine, next morning, when Piccola awoke. With one jump she was out on the floor and running toward the chimney. The shoe was lying where she had left it, but you could never, never guess what was in it.

Piccola had not meant to wake her mother, but this surprise was more than any little girl could bear and yet be quiet. She danced to the bed with the shoe in her hand, calling, 'Mother! Look! See the present Santa Claus brought me!'

Her mother raised her head and looked into the shoe. 'Why, Piccola,' she said, 'a little chimney swallow nestling in your shoe? What a good Santa Claus to bring you a bird!'

'Dear Santa Claus!' cried Piccola, and she kissed her mother and kissed the bird and kissed the shoe, and even threw kisses up the chimney, she was so happy.

When the bird was taken out of the shoe, they found that he did not try to fly, only to hop about the room. As they looked closer, they could see that one of his wings was hurt a little. Piccola's mother bound it up carefully. He took a drink of water from a cup, and even ate crumbs and seeds out of Piccola's hands.

She was a proud little girl when she took her Christmas present to show the children in the garden. They had had a great many gifts – dolls, bright picture books, cars and toy pianos; but not one of their playthings was alive, like Piccola's bird. They were as pleased as she, and Rose hunted about the house until she found a large wicker cage. She gave the cage to Piccola, and the swallow seemed to make himself quite at home in it at once. Rose had saved a bag of candies for Piccola, and when she went home at last, with the cage and her dear swallow safely inside it, I am sure there was not a happier little girl in the whole country of Italy.

SANTA CLAUS IN THE BUSH

Adapted from the Australian poem written by A. B. (Banjo) Paterson

It chanced out back at Christmas time,
When the wheat was ripe and tall,
A stranger rode to the farmer's gate –
A sturdy man, and small.

'Run down, run down, my little son Jack,
And bid the stranger stay;
And we'll have fun for old time's sake,
For the morn is Christmas Day.'

'Not now, not now,' said the dour good-wife,
'But you should let him be;
He's maybe only a drover chap
From the land o' the Darling Pea.

'With a drover's tales, and a drover's thirst
To drink the whole night through;
Or he's maybe a life insurance man
Who'll talk us black and blue.'

'Good wife, he's never a drover chap,
For their swags are neat and thin;
And he's never a life insurance man,
With the brick-dust burnt in his skin.

'You can set him a chair at the table side,
And give him a bite to eat;
An omelette made of a new-laid egg,
Or a tasty bit of meat.'

'A waste of food,' said the dour good-wife,
As she took the egg, with a frown,
'But he gets no meat, unless you run
A pademelon down.'

'Tis well, 'tis well,' said the bonny wee man;
'I have eaten the wide world's meat,
And the food that is given with right good will
Is the sweetest food to eat.

'But the night draws on to Christmas Day
And I must rise and go,
For I have a mighty way to ride
To the land of cold and snow.

'And it's there I must load my sledges up,
With reindeers four-in-hand,
That go to the north, south, east and west,
To each and every land.'

'To the cold and snow,' said the dour good-wife,
'You suit my husband well!
For when he gets up on his journey horse
He's a bit of a liar himself.'

Then out with a laugh went the bonny wee man
To his old horse grazing nigh,
And away like a meteor flash they went
Far off to the northern sky.

When the children woke on Christmas morn
They chattered with might and main,
For a ball and bat had little son Jack,
And a brand new doll had Jane,
And a packet of nails had husband John,
But the dour good-wife got none.

THE
FIRST
CHRISTMAS

THE STORY OF THE FIRST CHRISTMAS

Adapted from 'The Bible Story', written by Newton Marshall Hall and Irving Francis Wood

Once there were two little children who lived in a large red brick house on a quiet street in the city. Margaret was five years old, and Harold was eight. Margaret and Harold used to have the best of times together. They played with their dog Sport and their cat Spot. They built houses of blocks. They coloured pictures with their crayons. In winter, Harold pulled Margaret along on his sled, and in summer they played in the garden. But, better than all else, they loved to hear their mamma tell stories. Every night, before they went to bed, she told them a story.

'What shall it be tonight?' said Mamma, as they sat before the fire after a cold winter's day.

'A Bible story,' said Margaret.

'Very well,' replied Mamma. 'It shall be a Bible story tonight, and since it is almost Christmas time, I will tell you about the dear little Christ Child who was born in Bethlehem, and the first Christmas.'

So Margaret cuddled up in her mamma's lap, and Harold sat at her feet, and she began.

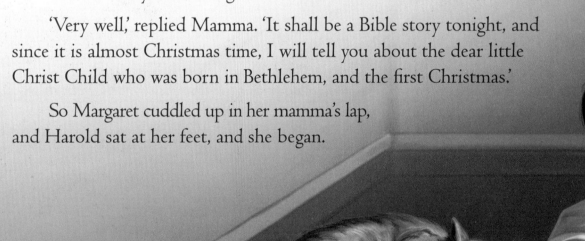

'Once upon a time, there was a little town called Bethlehem of Judea, and late one afternoon in winter, a man named Joseph and his wife named Mary came to this town. They were very glad to reach the village, for they were cold and hungry. But they were disappointed. No one could take them in. There is an old song that tells us about it:

' "O, dark was the night,
And cold blew the wind,
But Joseph and Mary
No shelter could find.

' "In all the fair city
Of Bethlehem,
In cottage or inn,
Was no room for them." '

'Wouldn't anyone let them in?' said Margaret.

'No,' said Mamma. 'They went to the inn, or hotel, of Bethlehem, and the keeper of the inn said, "No room for you here, we're full." They went to each one of the houses, and the people who lived in them said sadly, "No room for you here, we're sorry." '

'I would have let them in if I had been there,' said Harold, earnestly.

'I would, too,' said Margaret. 'Were they very cold, dear Mamma?'

'Yes, my dears,' said Mamma, smiling, 'I know that you would have been kind to them. But you see this was a busy time and every bed in the town was taken. Well, they were very cold and very sad, but at last the keeper of the inn let them go into his stable, and there were oxen there, and hay, and stalls for the cattle, and mangers.'

'Like Grandpapa's barn?' asked Harold.

'Yes,' answered Mamma, 'only not so nice and comfortable. That night, in the stable, the little baby Jesus was born, and his dear mother Mary wrapped him all warmly up, and laid him in one of the cattle mangers for a cradle.'

'And in the fields nearby there were shepherds keeping watch over their flocks by night, and while they watched they saw suddenly a great light, and an angel stood before them and said, "Be not afraid, for I bring you good tidings of great joy for all the people. For there is born in Bethlehem a little child Jesus, who is to be the Saviour of the world." And when the angel had finished speaking, they heard voices, singing like a great chorus in the sky, and this was the song they sang:

' "Glory to God in the highest,
And on earth peace among men in whom he is well pleased."

'Then the shepherds went to Bethlehem, and found the little child Jesus lying in the manger, and loved him, and told everyone what they had seen and heard.'

'And later, wise men from the East came on their three camels, guided by the star of Bethlehem, which shone in the sky. And as they came near to Bethlehem, they said to everyone, "Where is he who is born king? For we have seen his star in the East, and have come to worship him."

'And the star led them at last to the stable where Jesus was, and they brought beautiful gifts: gold, frankincense and myrrh, and they worshipped him.'

'And that is how Christmas came!' said Margaret. 'I am very glad that the little child Jesus was born.'

ONCE IN ROYAL DAVID'S CITY

Words by Cecil Frances Alexander

Once in royal David's city
Stood a lowly cattle shed,
Where a mother laid her baby
In a manger for His bed;
Mary was that mother mild,
Jesus Christ her little child.

He came down to earth from heaven,
Who is God and Lord of all,
And His shelter was a stable,
And His cradle was a stall;
With the poor, and mean, and lowly,
Lived on earth our Saviour holy.

And through all His wondrous childhood
He would honour and obey,
Love and watch the lowly Maiden
In whose gentle arms He lay;
Christian children all must be
Mild, obedient, good as He.

For He is our childhood's pattern;
Day by day, like us He grew;
He was little, weak and helpless,
Tears and smiles like us He knew;
And He feeleth for our sadness,
And He shareth in our gladness.

And our eyes at last shall see Him,
Through His own redeeming love;
For that Child so dear and gentle
Is our Lord in heaven above;
And He leads His children on
To the place where He is gone.

Not in that poor lowly stable,
With the oxen standing by,
We shall see Him; but in heaven,
Set at God's right hand on high;
Where like stars His children crowned
All in white shall wait around.

O LITTLE TOWN OF BETHLEHEM

Words by Phillips Brooks

O little town of Bethlehem,
How still we see thee lie!
Above thy deep and dreamless sleep
The silent stars go by.
Yet in thy dark streets shineth
The everlasting light;
The hopes and fears of all the years
Are met in thee tonight.

O morning stars, together
Proclaim the holy birth!
And praises sing to God the King,
And peace to men on earth.
For Christ is born of Mary
And gathered all above,
While mortals sleep the angels keep
Their watch of wondering love.

How silently, how silently,
The wondrous gift is given!
So God imparts to human hearts
The blessings of His Heaven.
No ear may hear His coming;
But in this world of sin,
Where meek souls will receive Him still
The dear Christ enters in.

Where children pure and happy
Pray to the blessed Child,
Where Misery cries out to Thee,
Son of the Mother mild;
Where Charity stands watching,
And Faith holds wide the door,
The dark night wakes, the glory breaks,
And Christmas comes once more.

O holy Child of Bethlehem!
Descend to us we pray!
Cast out our sin and enter in,
Be born in us today.
We hear the Christmas angels
The great glad tidings tell;
O, come to us, abide with us,
Our Lord Emmanuel!

INFANT HOLY, INFANT LOWLY

Traditional Polish carol

Infant holy, infant lowly, for His bed a cattle stall;
Oxen lowing, little knowing, Christ the Babe is Lord of all.
Swift are winging, angels singing, noels ringing, tidings bringing,
Christ the Babe is Lord of all.

Flocks were sleeping, shepherds keeping vigil till the morning new,
Saw the glory, heard the story, tidings of a Gospel true.
Thus rejoicing, free from sorrow, praises voicing, greet the morrow,
Christ the Babe was born for you.

AWAY IN A MANGER

Traditional carol

Away in a manger,
No crib for a bed,
The little Lord Jesus,
Laid down His sweet head.

The stars in the bright sky,
Looked down where He lay,
The little Lord Jesus,
Asleep on the hay.

The cattle are lowing,
The poor Baby wakes,
But little Lord Jesus,
No crying He makes.

I love Thee, Lord Jesus,
Look down from the sky,
And stay by my side,
'Til morning is nigh.

Be near me, Lord Jesus,
I ask Thee to stay,
Close by me forever,
And love me I pray.

Bless all the dear children,
In Thy tender care,
And fit us for heaven,
To live with Thee there.

THE FRIENDLY BEASTS

Traditional English carol

Jesus our brother, kind and good
Was humbly born in a stable rude
And the friendly beasts around Him stood,
Jesus our brother, kind and good.

'I,' said the donkey, shaggy and brown,
'I carried His mother up hill and down;
I carried her safely to Bethlehem town.'
'I,' said the donkey, shaggy and brown.

'I,' said the cow all white and red,
'I gave Him my manger for His bed;
I gave Him my hay to pillow His head.'
'I,' said the cow all white and red.

'I,' said the sheep with curly horn,
'I gave Him my wool for His blanket warm;
He wore my coat on Christmas morn.'
'I,' said the sheep with curly horn.

'I,' said the dove from the rafters high,
'I cooed Him to sleep so He would not cry;
We cooed Him to sleep, my mate and I.'
'I,' said the dove from the rafters high.

Thus every beast by some good spell,
In the stable dark was glad to tell
Of the gift he gave Emmanuel,
The gift he gave Emmanuel.

'I,' was glad to tell
Of the gift he gave Emmanuel,
The gift he gave Emmanuel.
Jesus our brother, kind and good.

WHILE SHEPHERDS WATCHED THEIR FLOCKS BY NIGHT

Words by Nahum Tate and Nicholas Brody

While shepherds watched
their flocks by night,
All seated on the ground,
The angel of the Lord came down,
And glory shone around.

'Fear not,' he said, for mighty dread
Had seized their troubled minds.
'Glad tidings of great joy I bring
To you and all mankind.

'To you in David's town, this day
Is born of David's line
The Saviour who is Christ the Lord,
And this shall be the sign.

'The heavenly Babe you there shall find
To human view displayed,
All meanly wrapped in swaddling bands,
And in a manger laid.'

Thus spake the seraph, and forthwith
Appeared a shining throng
Of angels praising God, who thus
Addressed their joyful song.

'All glory be to God on high,
And to the earth be peace;
Goodwill henceforth from heaven to men
Begin and never cease!'

GOD REST YOU MERRY, GENTLEMEN

Traditional carol

God rest you merry, gentlemen,
Let nothing you dismay,
For Jesus Christ our Saviour
Was born upon this day,
To save us all from Satan's power
When we were gone astray.

Chorus

O tidings of comfort and joy,
Comfort and joy,
O tidings of comfort and joy.

In Bethlehem, in Israel,
This blessèd Babe was born,
And laid within a manger
Upon this blessèd morn,
The which His Mother Mary
Did nothing take in scorn.

Chorus

From God our heavenly Father
A blessèd angel came,
And unto certain shepherds
Brought tidings of the same,
How that in Bethlehem was born
The Son of God by name.

Chorus

The shepherds at those tidings
Rejoicèd much in mind,
And left their flocks a-feeding
In tempest, storm and wind,
And went to Bethlehem straightway,
This blessèd Babe to find.

Chorus

But when to Bethlehem they came,
Whereat this Infant lay,
They found Him in a manger,
Where oxen feed on hay;
His mother Mary kneeling,
Unto the Lord did pray.

Chorus

Now to the Lord sing praises,
All you within this place,
And with true love and brotherhood
Each other now embrace;
This holy tide of Christmas
Doth bring redeeming grace.

Chorus

O Holy Night!

Words by John Sullivan Dwight

O holy night, the stars are brightly shining,
It is the night of the dear Saviour's birth.
Long lay the world in sin and error pining,
Till He appeared and the soul felt its worth.
A thrill of hope, the weary world rejoices,
For yonder breaks a new and glorious morn.

    Fall on your knees! O hear the angel voices!
    O night divine, O night when Christ was born;
    O night, O holy night, O night divine!

Led by the light of faith serenely beaming,
With glowing hearts by His cradle we stand.
So led by light of a star sweetly gleaming,
Here come the Wise Men from Orient land.
The King of kings lay thus in lowly manger;
In all our trials born to be our friend.

    He knows our need, to our weakness is no stranger,
    Behold your King! Before him lowly bend!
    Behold your King! Before him lowly bend!

Truly He taught us to love one another,
His law is love and His gospel is peace.
Chains shall He break, for the slave is our brother,
And in His name all oppression shall cease.
Sweet hymns of joy in grateful chorus raise we,
Let all within us praise His holy name.

    Christ is the Lord! O praise His name forever,
    His power and glory evermore proclaim!
    His power and glory evermore proclaim!

THE FIRST NOEL

Traditional carol

The first Noel the angels did say,
Was to certain poor shepherds in fields as they lay;
In fields where they lay keeping their sheep,
On a cold winter's night that was so deep.

Chorus

Noel, Noel, Noel, Noel,
Born is the King of Israel.

They looked up and saw a star,
Shining in the east, beyond them far;
And to the earth it gave great light,
And so it continued both day and night.

Chorus

And by the light of that same star,
Three Wise Men came from country far;
To seek for a King was their intent,
And to follow the star wherever it went.

Chorus

This star drew nigh to the north-west,
O'er Bethlehem it took its rest;
And there it did both stop and stay,
Right over the place where Jesus lay.

Chorus

Then entered in those Wise Men three,
Fell reverently upon their knee;
And offered there in his presence,
Their gold and myrrh and frankincense.

Chorus

Then let us all with one accord,
Sing praises to our heavenly Lord;
That hath made heaven and earth of naught,
And with his blood mankind hath bought.

Chorus

WHAT CHILD IS THIS?

Words by William Chatterton Dix

What child is this, who, laid to rest,
On Mary's lap is sleeping,
Whom angels greet with anthems sweet,
While shepherds watch are keeping?
This, this is Christ the King,
Whom shepherds guard and angels sing;
Haste, haste to bring Him praise,
The Babe, the Son of Mary!

Why lies He in such mean estate,
Where ox and ass are feeding?
Come, have no fear; God's son is here.
His love all loves exceeding.
Nails, spear shall pierce Him through,
The Cross He bore for me, for you;
Hail, hail, the Saviour comes,
The Babe, the Son of Mary!

So bring Him incense, gold and myrrh;
Come, peasant, king, to own Him!
The King of kings salvation brings;
Let loving hearts enthrone Him!
Raise, raise the song on high!
While Mary sings a lullaby.
Joy, joy, for Christ is born,
The Babe, the Son of Mary!

SILENT NIGHT

Words by Joseph Mohr

Silent night, holy night,
All is calm, all is bright
Round yon virgin mother and Child.
Holy Infant, so tender and mild,
Sleep in heavenly peace,
Sleep in heavenly peace.

Silent night, holy night,
Shepherds quake at the sight;
Glories stream from heaven afar,
Heavenly hosts sing Alleluia!
Christ, the Saviour is born,
Christ, the Saviour is born!

Silent night, holy night,
Son of God, love's pure light;
Radiant beams from Thy holy face
With the dawn of redeeming grace,
Jesus, Lord, at Thy birth,
Jesus, Lord, at Thy birth.

O Come All Ye Faithful

English translation by Frederick Oakeley

O come, all ye faithful,
Joyful and triumphant,
O come ye, O come ye to Bethlehem.
Come and behold Him, born the King of angels.

Chorus

O come, let us adore Him,
O come, let us adore Him,
O come, let us adore Him,
Christ the Lord.

O Sing, choirs of angels,
Sing in exultation,
Sing all that hear in heaven God's holy word.
Give to our Father glory in the Highest.

Chorus

All Hail! Lord, we greet Thee,
Born this happy morning,
O Jesus! For evermore be Thy name adored.
Word of the Father, now in flesh appearing.

Chorus

JOY TO THE WORLD

Words by Isaac Watts

Joy to the world! The Lord is come!
Let earth receive her King;
Let every heart prepare Him room,
And heaven and nature sing,
And heaven and nature sing,
And heaven, and heaven, and nature sing.

Joy to the Earth! The Saviour reigns!
Let men their songs employ;
While fields and floods, rocks, hills, and plains
Repeat the sounding joy,
Repeat the sounding joy,
Repeat, repeat the sounding joy.

No more let sins and sorrows grow,
Nor thorns infest the ground;
He comes to make His blessings flow
Far as the curse is found,
Far as the curse is found,
Far as, far as, the curse is found.

He rules the world with truth and grace,
And makes the nations prove
The glories of His righteousness,
And wonders of His love,
And wonders of His love,
And wonders, wonders, of His love.

HARK! THE HERALD ANGELS SING

Words by Charles Wesley

Hark! The herald angels sing,
'Glory to the newborn King!
Peace on earth, and mercy mild,
God and sinners reconciled!'
Joyful, all ye nations rise,
Join the triumph of the skies;
With th' angelic host proclaim,
'Christ is born in Bethlehem!'

Chorus

Hark! The herald angels sing,
'Glory to the newborn King!'

Christ, by highest heav'n adored;
Christ, the everlasting Lord!
Late in time behold Him come,
Offspring of a virgin's womb.
Veiled in flesh the Godhead see;
Hail th' incarnate Deity,
Pleased with us in flesh to dwell,
Jesus, our Emmanuel.

Chorus

Hail the heav'n-born Prince of Peace!
Hail the Son of Righteousness!
Light and life to all He brings,
Ris'n with healing in His wings.
Mild He lays His glory by,
Born that we no more may die,
Born to raise us from the earth,
Born to give us second birth.

Chorus